THE BRIDE
WORE BLACK

CORNELL WOOLRICH (1903–1968) was one of America's best crime and noir writers, who also published under the names George Hopley and William Irish. His novels were among the first to employ the atmosphere, outlook, and impending sense of doom that came to be characterized as noir, and inspired some of the most famous films of the period, including *Rear Window*, *The Phantom Lady*, *The Leopard Man*, *Black Angel*, and many, many more.

EDDIE MULLER, "The Czar of Noir," is the founder and president of the Film Noir Foundation, and provides commentary for noir films and specials on Turner Classic Movies. He created his own graphics firm, St. Francis Studio, and is the author of *Grindhouse*, *Dark City Dames*, and *Dark City*. He lives in the San Francisco Bay Area.

THE BRIDE WORE BLACK

CORNELL WOOLRICH

Introduction by
EDDIE MULLER

AMERICAN MYSTERY CLASSICS

Penzler Publishers
New York

Published in 2021 by Penzler Publishers
58 Warren Street, New York, NY 10007
penzlerpublishers.com

Distributed by W. W. Norton

Cover image: Andy Ross
Cover design: Mauricio Diaz

Paperback ISBN 9781613162002
Hardcover ISBN 9781613161999

Library of Congress Control Number: 2020921102

Printed in the United States of America

9 8 7 6 5 4 3 2 1

THE BRIDE
WORE BLACK

INTRODUCTION

H<small>E DEDICATED IT</small> to a typewriter. And the mysterious CHULA, whomever or whatever that may be. The first novel in Cornell Woolrich's prodigious outpouring of literary fear and paranoia is dedicated to an enigma and an inanimate object. Appropriate, considering the life lived by America's greatest writer of suspense. His relentless use of Remington Portable No. NC69411, the incessant pounding and cajoling of its keys, was the most intimate relationship in the poor, lonely bastard's life. Woolrich invested everything he had in the marriage.

The Bride Wore Black, published in 1940, was not technically Woolrich's first novel. He'd scored an early success in 1927 with *Children of the Ritz*, a Roaring Twenties, F. Scott Fitzgerald knockoff that gave no indication of the horrors to come. It wasn't until Woolrich began churning out short stories for the pulps that his unique style and nihilistic worldview emerged. *Bride* was the first in his legendary series of "Black" novels (*The Black Curtain*, *Black Alibi*, *The Black Angel*, *The Black Path of Fear*, and *Rendezvous in Black*) that would make him, through sales of the stories to the movies, radio, and television, the most financially successful "pulp" writer ever. Yet Woolrich lived like a pauper, stepping away from the Remington only long enough to pour copious amounts of restorative booze into his spindly frame.

"All I was trying to do was cheat death." That's how he described his writing career. I've always been haunted by a passage from Woolrich's never-published-in-his-lifetime autobiography, *Blues of a Lifetime*, in which he recalled being a young boy living with his father in Mexico: ". . . when I was eleven and, huddling over my own knees, looking up at the low-hanging stars of the Valley of Anahuac, and I knew I would surely die finally, or something worse. . . . I had that trapped feeling, like some sort of poor insect that you've put inside a downturned glass, and it tries to climb up the sides, and it can't, and it can't, and it can't." A moment of existential dread that foretold his literary legacy.

Woolrich's biographer, Francis M. Nevins, declared the writer's life the most wretched of any American writer since Edgar Allan Poe—although the facts of that life are as elusive as smoke. Woolrich was a compulsive liar, always rewriting facts to tell a better story. We do know, thanks to Nevins' research, that Woolrich was a self-loathing gay man whose lifelong residency in a locked closet no doubt contributed to the secrecy and paranoia that drips from his stories. The real man may be the sum of what he left on the page, a writer who assembled his neuroses into breathless communiques from a lonely outpost in the Hotel Marseille, Broadway at 103rd in Manhattan, which he shared with his mother, Claire. From his upper-floor apartment, he surveyed the city's roofs and alleys and fire escapes, imagining the myriad terrors that could befall souls streaming through the city's clogged arteries. Then he set upon Remington No.

NC69411 and, like a mad conductor, summoned the music of desire and dread.

Woolrich was the most noir writer in the mystery genre, as *The Bride Wore Black* amply proves. It contains all the requisite elements: the obsessive protagonist on a murderous quest, the latticework of dreadful coincidence, the relentless (and strangely exhilarating) spiral into madness, the *denouement* that twists the knife an extra turn. This was Woolrich's métier, and it led to his stories and novels being grist for dozens of films—few of which captured the writer's special combination of dread, delirium, and breathless suspense. François Truffaut's 1968 adaptation of *The Bride Wore Black* used the book merely as a tool to emulate and idolize Alfred Hitchcock. The result was an aloof genre exercise lacking the book's excitement and empathy.

Although he was one of the most prolific mystery writers of all time, Woolrich never earned the literary cachet of contemporaries like Dashiell Hammett and Raymond Chandler (who also emerged from the pages of *Black Mask*) or James M. Cain, whose slim and nasty novels (particularly *The Postman Always Rings Twice* and *Double Indemnity*) are credited with setting the template for noir. Compared to Woolrich, the output of those three legends was meager. Woolrich's hundreds of stories, taken individually, are nerve-jangling diversions; as a life's work they added up to towering wall of existential malevolence not even Sartre or Camus would dare to scale.

Literary critics, of course, were always disdainful of Woolrich. His stories are not conducive to analysis or interpretation. He was not an elegant writer. You don't re-read him for the beauty of the prose. His work should not be intellectualized—it should be consumed, in a feverish rush. That's how you feel the undertow, surrendering to the rush of words, carried away on the relentless black tide. Chandler called Woolrich the best "idea man" in the business, even though his plots invariably turn on credulity-stretching coincidences, which rankles those readers who demand logic and realism.

To which I say, "Since when are nightmares logical?"

—EDDIE MULLER

THE BRIDE
WORE BLACK

To
CHULA
and
Remington Portable No. NC69411
in
unequal parts.

For to kill is the great law set by nature in the heart of existence!
There is nothing more beautiful and honorable than killing!
—DE MAUPASSANT

PART ONE

BLISS

Blue moon, you saw me standing alone,
Without a dream in my heart, without a love of my own.
Blue moon, you knew just what I was there for. . . .

RODGERS AND HART

I

The Woman

"JULIE, MY JULIE." It followed the woman down the four flights of the stairwell. It was the softest whisper, the strongest claim, that human lips can utter. It did not make her falter, lose a step. Her face was white when she came out into the daylight, that was all.

The girl waiting by the valise at the street entrance turned and looked at her almost incredulously as she joined her, as though wondering where she had found the fortitude to go through with it. The woman seemed to read her thoughts; she answered the unspoken question. "It was just as hard for me to say goodbye as for them, only I was used to it, they weren't. I had so many long nights in which to steel myself. They only went through it once; I've had to go through it a thousand times." And without any change of tone, she went on, "I'd better take a taxi. There's one down there."

The girl looked at her questioningly as it drew up.

"Yes, you can see me off if you want. To the Grand Central Station, driver."

She didn't look back at the house, at the street they were

leaving. She didn't look out at the many other well-remembered streets that followed, that in their aggregate stood for her city, the place where she had always lived.

They had to wait a moment at the ticket window; there was somebody else before them. The girl stood helplessly by at her elbow. "Where are you going?"

"I don't even know, even at this very moment. I haven't thought about it until now." She opened her handbag, separated the small roll of currency it contained into two unequal parts; retained the smaller in her hand. She moved up before the window, thrust it in.

"How far will this take me, at day-coach rates?"

"Chicago—with ninety cents change."

"Then give me a one-way ticket." She turned to the girl beside her. "Now you can go back and tell them that much, at least."

"I won't if you don't want me to, Julie."

"It doesn't matter. What difference does the name of a place make when you're gone beyond recall?"

They sat for a while in the waiting room. Then presently they went below to the lower track level, stood for a moment by the coach doorway.

"We'll kiss, as former childhood friends should." Their lips met briefly. "There."

"Julie, what can I say to you?"

"Just 'goodbye.' What else is there to say to anyone ever—in this life?"

"Julie, I only hope I see you someday soon."

"You never will again."

The station platform fell behind. The train swept through the long tunnel. Then it emerged into daylight again, to ride an elevated trestle flush with the upper stories of tenements, while the crosswise streets ticked by like picket openings in a fence.

It started to slow again, almost before it had got fully under way. "Twanny-fith Street," droned a conductor into the car. The woman who had gone away forever seized her valise, stood up and walked down the aisle as though this were the end of the trip instead of the beginning.

She was standing in the vestibule, in readiness, when it drew up. She got off, walked along the platform to the exit, down the stairs to street level. She bought a paper at the waiting-room newsstand, sat down on one of the benches, opened the paper toward the back, to the classified ads. She furled it to a convenient width, traced a finger down the column under the heading Furnished Rooms.

The finger stopped almost at random, without much regard for the details offered by what it rested on. She dug her nail into the spongy paper, marking it. She tucked the newspaper under one arm, picked up her valise once more, walked outside to a taxi. "Take me to this address, here," she said, and showed him the paper.

The landlady at the furnished rooming house stood back, waiting for her verdict, by the open room door.

The woman turned around. "Yes, this will do very nicely. I'll give you the amount for the first two weeks now."

The landlady counted it, began to scribble a receipt. "What name, please?" she asked, looking up.

The woman's eyes flicked past her own valise with the "J.B." once initialed in gilt still dimly visible midway between the two latches. "Josephine Bailey."

"Here's your receipt, Miss Bailey. Now I hope you're comfortable. The bathroom's just two doors down the hall on your——"

"Thank you, thank you, I'll find out." She closed the door, locked it on the inside. She took off her hat and coat, opened her valise, so recently packed for a trip of fifty blocks—or a lifetime.

There was a small rust-flaked tin medicine cabinet tacked up above the washbowl. She went over to it and opened it, rising on her toes as though in search of something. On the topmost shelf, as she had half hoped, there was a rusted razor blade, left behind by some long-forgotten masculine roomer.

She went back to the valise with it, cut a little oblong around the initials on the lid, peeled off the top layer of the papier-mâché thus removing them bodily. Then she prodded through the contents of the receptacle, gashing at the stitching of an undergarment, a night robe, a blouse; removing those same two letters that had once stood for her wherever they were to be found.

Her predecessor obliterated, she threw the razor blade into the wastebasket, fastidiously wiped the tips of her fingers.

She found the picture of a man in the flap under the lid of the valise. She took it out and held it before her eyes, gazing at it for a long time. Just a young man, nothing wonderful about him: Not so strikingly handsome; just eyes and mouth and nose as anyone has. She looked at it a long time.

Then she found a folder of matches in her handbag and took the picture over to the washbasin. She touched a lighted match to one corner of it and held it until there was nothing to hold anymore.

"Goodbye," she breathed low.

She ran a spurt of water down through the basin and went back to the valise. All that was left now, in the flap under the lid, was a scrap of paper with a penciled name on it. It had taken a long time to get it. The woman looked further, took out four similar scraps.

She brought them all out. She didn't burn them right away. She played around with them first, as if in idle disinterest. She put them all down on the dresser top, blank sides up. Then she milled them around under her rotating fingertips. Then she picked one up, glanced briefly at the underside of it. Then she gathered them all together once more, burned all five of them alike over the washbowl.

Then she moved over toward the window, stood there looking out, a hand poised at each extremity of the slablike sill, gripping it. She seemed to *lean toward* the city visible outside, like something imminent, about to happen to it.

II

Bliss

THE CAB DREW up short at the entrance of Bliss's apartment house and threw him forward a little on the seat. The liquor in his stomach sloshed around with the jolt. Not because there was so much in him but because it was so recently absorbed.

He got out, and the top of the door frame knocked his hat askew. He straightened it, fumbled for change, dropped a dime to the sidewalk. He wasn't helplessly drunk; he never got that way. He knew everything that was said to him and everything he was saying, and he felt just right. Not too little, not too much. And then there was always the thought of Marge—it looked like he was getting someplace there. You didn't want to drown out a thought like that in liquor.

Charlie, on night door duty, came out behind him while he was paying the driver. Charlie was just a little behind time with his reception ritual, because he'd stayed behind on his bench in the foyer to finish the last paragraph of a sports writeup in a tabloid before coming out. But it was two-thirty in the morning, after all, and no one's perfect.

Bliss turned and said, "'Lo, Charlie."

Charlie answered, "Morning, Mr. Bliss." He held the entrance door open for him, and Bliss went inside. Charlie followed, his duties more or less satisfactorily performed. He yawned, and then Bliss caught it from him, without having seen him do it, and yawned, too—a fact that would have interested a metaphysician.

There was a mirror panel on one side of the lobby, and Bliss stepped up, took one of his usual going-in looks at himself. There were two kinds. The "boy-I-feel-swell, I-wonder-what's-up-tonight" look. That was the going out look. Then there was the "God-I-feel-terrible, be-glad-to-get-to-bed" look. That was the coming-back look.

Bliss saw a man of twenty-seven with close-cropped sandy hair, looking back at him. So close-cropped it looked silvery at the sides. Brown eyes, spare figure, good height without being too tall about it. A man who knew all about him—Bliss. Not handsome, but then who wanted to be handsome? Even Marge Elliott didn't care if he was handsome or not. "As long," as she had put it, "as you're just Ken."

He sighed, snapped his thumbnail at the bedraggled white flower that still clung to his lapel button-hole, and it flew to pieces.

Bliss took out a crumpled package of cigarettes, helped himself to one, scanned the neat hole in the upper right-hand corner. He saw that there was one left, offered it to Charlie. "Greater love hath no man," he remarked.

Charlie took it, perhaps figuring there wasn't likely to be anyone else coming in after this.

Charlie was big and roundish at the middle. He wasn't so good at polishing all the way down toward the bottom of the brass stanchions that supported the door canopy, but the middle and upper parts always shone like jewels, and he could handle twice his weight in disorderly drunks. He'd been night doorman in the building ever since Bliss had first moved into it. Bliss liked him. Charlie liked Bliss, too. Bliss gave him two bucks on Christmas and spread another two throughout the year in four-bit pieces. But that wasn't the reason; Charlie just liked him.

Bliss lit the two of them up. Then he turned and started up the two shallow steps to the self-service elevator. Charlie said, "Oh, I nearly forgot, Mr. Bliss. There was a young lady around to see you tonight."

"Yeah? What name'd she leave?" Bliss answered indifferently. It hadn't been Marge, so it really didn't matter much—anymore. He stopped and turned his face only a quarter of the way toward the answer.

"None," said Charlie. "I couldn't get her to leave any. I asked her two or three times, but—" he shrugged "—she didn't seem to want to."

"All right," said Bliss. And it *was* all right.

"She seemed to want to go upstairs and wait for you in the apartment," Charlie added.

"Oh, no, don't ever do that," Bliss said briskly. "Those days are over."

"I know. No, I wouldn't, Mr. Bliss, don't ever worry . . ." Charlie said with impressive sincerity. Then he added with a somewhat reticent shake of his head, "She sure wanted to bad, though."

Something about the way he said it aroused Bliss's curiosity. "Whaddya mean?" He dropped one foot down a step to the lower level again, turned head and shoulders more fully toward Charlie.

"Well, she was standing here with me, a little to one side,

over there by the mirror, after I'd already rung your announcer without getting any answer, and she said, 'Well, could I go up and wait?' I said, 'Well, I dunno, Miss. I'm not supposed to. . . .' You know, trying to let her down easy. And then she opened this bag, this evening pockybook she was holding on to, and sort of hunted around down in it like she was looking for a lipstick. And right there on top of all her things there was this hundred-dollar bill staring me in the face. Now y'may not want to believe me, Mr. Bliss, but I saw it with my own eyes——"

Bliss chuckled with good-natured derision. "And you think she was trying to offer you that to let her up, is that it? G'wan, Charlie." He kicked up one elbow scoffingly.

Nothing could lessen Charlie's pained, round-eyed earnestness. "I *know* she was for a fact, Mr. Bliss, y'couldn't miss it, the way she done it. She left the top of the bag wide open and went around under it with her fingers, so's to be sure not to disturb it. It was spread out flat, see, on top of everything else. Then she looked from it to me, looked me square in the eye—even holding the bag a little ways out from her. Not right *at* me, y'understand, but just a little ways out, so I'd catch on what she meant. Listen, I been in this business long enough. I know all the signs. I could *tell*."

Bliss scratched the corner of his mouth reflectively with the cutting edge of one thumbnail, as if feeling to see if it was still there. "Are you sure it wasn't just a ten spot, Charlie?"

Charlie's voice became almost falsetto in its aggrieved insistence. "Mr.

Bliss, I *seen* the two O's in both upper corners of it!"

Bliss worried his lip between the edge of his teeth, pinching it in. "Well, I'll be damned!" He turned full body toward Charlie at last, as though intending to talk until this thing had been thrashed out to his satisfaction.

Charlie seemed to understand the need for further colloquy between the two of them. He said, "Be right with you, Mr. Bliss," as the sound of another cab arriving outside reached them. He went out, did his devoir with the doors, returned in the wake of a man and woman in evening garb who must have been very spruce at eight-thirty. All the starch was out of them now.

They nodded slightly to Bliss in passing, and he nodded slightly back to them, with all the awful frigidity of metropolitan neighbors. They stepped into the car and went up.

As soon as the glass porthole in the elevator panel had blacked out, Charlie and he resumed where they had left off. "Well, what'd she look like? Was she anyone you ever saw before? You know most of the crowd I used to have around to see me pretty well."

"Yes, I do," Charlie admitted. "And I can't place her. I'm sure I never seen her before, Mr. Bliss, all I can tell you is she was some looker. Was she some looker!"

"All right, she was some looker," agreed Bliss, "but like what?"

"Well, she was blond." Charlie brought his hands into play as the artist in him came to the fore. He outlined—presumably—masses of luxuriant hair. "But this *real* blond, y'know this real yella blond? Not this phony, washed-out, silvery kind they make it. This real blond."

"This real blond," Bliss confirmed patiently.

"And—and blue eyes; y'know, the kind that are always laughing, even when they're not? And about this high—her chin came up to this second chevron here, on me sleeve, see? And, er, not too fat, but y'wouldn't call her skinny, either; just a right armful——"

Bliss was eying the far side of the foyer ceiling as the description unfolded. "No," he kept saying, "no," as if going over the records himself. "The closest I can come to it is Helen Raymond, but——"

"No, I 'member Miss Raymond," Charlie said firmly. "It wasn't her; I got a cab for her many a time." Then he said, "Anyway, y'know how I'm pretty sure you don't know her? Because she didn't know you herself."

"*What?*" said Bliss, "Then what the hell did she want coming around asking for me, trying to get into my place?"

Charlie was still a lap behind him in the circles they seemed to be making. "She didn't know you worth a damn," he repeated with heavy emphasis. "I tried her out, on the way up——"

"Oh, so then you *were* going to let her up. That must have been a hundred, after all."

Charlie cleared his throat deprecatingly, realizing he had made a faux pas. "No, Mr. Bliss, no," he protested soulfully. "Now, you know me better than that; I wasn't. But I did start up on the car with her, acting like I was going to. I thought maybe that'd be the quickest way of getting rid of her, pretend like I was going to and then at the last minute——"

"Yeah, I know," said Bliss dryly.

"Well, we started up in the car together, to the fourth. And on the way I remembered that robbery we had here in the building last year, y'know, and I figured I better not take any chances. So I started to reel her out a fake description of you, just the opposite of your real one to try her out. I said, 'He's red-headed, ain't he, and pretty tall, just a little bit under six feet? I'm kind of new on the job here. I wanna make sure I got him placed right, there are so many tenants in the building.' She fell for it like a ton of bricks. 'Yes, of course,' she said, 'that's him.' Kind of quickly, to keep me from catching on that was the first time she heard what you looked like herself."

"Well, I'll be a—" Bliss said. He went ahead and said what it was he would be.

"So, of course, that was enough for me," Charlie assured him virtuously. "That finished it. When I heard that I said to myself, 'Nothing doing. Not on my shift, y'don't!' But I didn't say anything to her, because—well, she was dressed pretty swell and all that, not the kind it pays to get tough with. So I let her down easy, tried the wrong key to your door and when it wouldn't work pretended I didn't have no other and couldn't let her in. We went downstairs again, and she just kind of shrugged it off, like if she hadn't gotten in that time, it didn't matter because she was going to sooner or later. She smiled and said, 'Some other time, then,' and started off down the street, just the way she came walking. It was funny, too, dressed up the way she was. I watched her as far as the corner, and I didn't see her call no cab or nothing, just walked along like it was ten in the morning. Then she turned the corner and disappeared. O'Connor, the cop, he passed her coming up this way, and I even seen him turn and look after her. She sure was a looker."

"Just a ship that passes in the night," remarked Bliss. "Well, one sure thing, it was some kind of stall. If I didn't know her—and I don't, from your description—and she didn't know me, what was it all about? What the hell was she after? Maybe she had me mixed up with somebody else."

"No, she had your name right, even your first name. 'Mr. Ken Bliss,' she asked for when she first come in."

"And she didn't drive up, either, you say?"

"No, just came walking along from nowhere, then went walking away again just like she came. Funniest thing I ever seen."

They talked it over a few moments longer, man to man, with the typical freemasonry of two-thirty in the morning. "Aw, you run into a lot of funny things like that from time to time, livin' in a big city like this. You're bound to. I know, Mr. Bliss, I seen enough of them myself, in my line of work. Nuts that think they know you, and nuts that think they love you, and nuts that think you done something to them. You'd be surprised what bugs and mental cases there are walking around loose——"

"So now maybe I've got one of 'em fastened on me. That's a cheerful thought to take up to bed," Bliss grimaced.

He turned away, readied the elevator panel. He flashed Charlie a mock-apprehensive backward grin just before it closed on him. "It's getting so a young guy ain't safe anymore living by himself. I think I'll get myself married off and get hold of some protection!"

But the thought that he took up with him was of Marjorie— not of anyone else.

Corey showed up at his door at eight-thirty, long before he'd even begun to get ready, the night of Marjorie's engagement party. "What the hell," Bliss said with the pretended disgruntlement one shows only a close friend, "I only just got back from eating; I haven't even shaved yet."

"I called y'at the office at four-thirty. Where the hell

were you?" Corey barked back at him with equally familiar brusqueness.

He came in and appropriated the best chair, swung one leg up over its arm. He got rid of his hat by aiming it at the windowsill. It missed but stayed on a low book rack underneath.

Corey wasn't a bad-looking sort of fellow, without being decorative about it. Taller than Bliss, a little leaner—or maybe just seeming so because he was taller—and with dark brown hair and heavy brows. He tried to be man-about-townish in an *Esquire* sort of way, but it was just a veneer; you could tell he was a primitive underneath that. Every once in a while a crack would show, and you'd get a startling glimpse of jungle through it. Veneer or not, he worked hard at it. Any party you ever went to he was there, holding up a door frame, hand-warming a glass. Any girl you ever mentioned him to, she knew him, too—or had a friend who did. His technique was a head-on attack, a blitzkrieg, and it had succeeded in the unlikeliest quarters. Some of the haughtiest, most unbending shoulders in town had been pinned to the mat, if the truth had only been known.

He started rubbing his hands with a fine show of malicious glee. "Well, tonight you get hooked! Tonight you get branded! Feel like running out yet? You bet you do! You're all white around the gills——"

"Think I'm like you?"

Corey trip-hammered a thumb against his own chest. "You should be like me. This is one guy they don't pin down to a formal promise!"

"If you'd bathed oftener, maybe you'd get more offers," Bliss grunted disparagingly.

"And make them have a hard time finding me when the

lights go out? That wouldn't be fair. So where were you this afternoon? I wanted to eat with you."

"I was out getting the headlight. Where d'you suppose?" He
opened a dresser drawer, took out a little cubed box, snapped
the lid. "What d'you think of it?"

Corey took it out of the plush, breathed on it admiringly.
"Say, is that a rock!"

"It ought to be. It threw me pul-lenty." Bliss pitched it back
in the drawer with an air of indifference that was admirably as-
sumed, started unhitching his suspenders. "I'm going in and
take a shower. You know where the Scotch is."

He came in again in something under twenty minutes, complete down to bat-wing tie. "Who was the dame?" Corey asked
idly, looking up from a newspaper.

"What dame?"

"The phone rang just now while you were in there, and some
girl asked for you. I could tell it wasn't one of your old pals by
the way she spoke. 'Does Mr. Kenneth Bliss live there?' I told
her you were busy and asked if there was anything I could do.
Not another word, just hung up."

"Strange."

Corey swiveled his drink. "Maybe it was one of these women
society reporters looking for stuff on your engagement."

"No, they usually tackle the girl end of it. Marjorie's people
have already given out all the dope there is, anyway. I wonder if
it was *her?*" he said after a moment's thought.

"Who's her?"

Bliss grinned. "I haven't told you but I think I've got a secret admirer. Funny thing happened not long ago. One night
when I was out a beautiful girl tried her level best to get into
the apartment here. The doorman told me about it afterward.

She wouldn't give her name or anything. He knows most of the crowd I used to hang out with—you know how doormen get after a while—and he was pretty sure he'd never seen her before. She was all togged out in evening clothes, looked like real carriage trade to his practiced eye. But she didn't drive up to the door, that was the strangest part of it; just came strolling along the street from nowhere, dressed to kill like that.

"He told me she opened her bag, pretending to hunt for a lipstick or something, and let him get a good look at a hundred-dollar bill floating around on top of everything else. And the way she acted gave him a pretty good idea it would have been his for the asking if he'd just opened my door with his passkey and let her in."

Corey looked skeptical. "You mean a doorman is going to turn down a chance to make a hundred dollars that easy? He's bulling you."

"I don't know about that. The amount is so fantastic in itself that, to me at any rate, it bears the earmark of truth. If he was just making the thing up, he would have been more likely to make it ten or twenty dollars."

"Well, what'd he do—let her in?"

"I could tell by the way he spoke that the hundred darned near got him; he was just on the point of bringing her up and letting her in. Only he thought he'd better try her out first, see if she really knew me, before he went ahead and admitted her. So he strung her along with a fake description that was just the opposite of mine in every respect, and she fell for it, said yes, that was the man—proving she'd never seen me before in her life.

"That finished it, of course; he was afraid to take a chance after that. He pretended he didn't have the key or something and eased her out as tactfully as he could. She was too well dressed for him to get snotty with. When she saw it was no go, she just smiled, shrugged and went sauntering down the street again."

Corey was leaning interestedly forward by this time. "And are you sure you don't recognize her from his description?"

"Dead sure. And as I just told you, she didn't recognize me, either."

"I wonder what she was after?"

"She wasn't out to clean the apartment, that's a cinch, because she was willing to pay a hundred dollars just for the privilege of getting in here, and anyone who can get a hundred dollars' worth out of this place is a magician."

Corey nodded judicious agreement on that point.

Bliss stood up. "Let's go." He smiled nervously. "I like everything about marriage except the functions leading up to it—such as tonight's."

"The part I like best," said Corey, "is not having it happen in the first place."

They were out in the public half waiting for the self-service car when a thin, querulous ringing piped up behind a closed door somewhere nearby.

Bliss cocked an experienced ear. "Key of G flat. That's mine. I'd better hop in and take it a minute; it may be Marge."

He went back to the door, fumbled in his pocket for his key, dropped it, had to stoop to get it. Corey stuck his foot out to hold the car up for them, "Hurry up before somebody gets it away from us," he urged.

Bliss pitched the door open. The thin wail rose to a full-toned peal, then perversely stopped short and didn't resume. He backed out again, pulled the door shut after him. "Too late, they've quit trying."

Riding down in the elevator, Corey suggested, "Maybe it was that same mystery dame again."

"If it was," Bliss grunted, "whatever it is she wants, she sure wants bad."

Alone there with Marge, in a little alcove away from the rest of the party, he scratched the back of his neck in pretended perplexity. "Let's see now, how does this go? I've seen enough movies, I ought to have the hang of it. Well, let's give it the old shut-eye treatment, that's the safest. Shut your eyes and stick out your finger.

She promptly hooked her thumb toward him.

He slapped it out of the way. "Not *that* one. Help a fellow out. I'm so nervous I could——"

"Oh, wrong finger? You should be more specific. How'd I know but what you wanted to bite it or something?"

And then the ring. Their heads drew together, looking down at it; they made a love knot of their four hands. They made nonsensical purrings and cooings and other noises that to them were probably language. Suddenly both became aware of eyes regarding them steadfastly, and they turned their heads in unison toward the doorway. A girl was outlined in it, as motionless as though she had taken root in the floor.

She was in tiered, wide-spreading black, the creamy whiteness of her shoulders rising out of it without any interrupting straps. A gossamer black wimple twinkling with jet was drawn over hair so incredibly yellow it seemed to have been powdered with corneal.

A dimple of sympathy—or possibly derision—at the corner of her mouth had disappeared before they could confirm it. "Pardon me," she said quietly, and moved on.

"What a striking girl!" Marjorie exclaimed involuntarily, continuing to stare at the empty doorway as though hypnotized. "Who is she?"

"I don't know. I think I remember her coming in along with Fred Sterling and his party, but if I was introduced, it didn't take."

They looked down at the ring once more. But the spell had been broken, their mood was gone, they couldn't seem to get it back. The room didn't feel quite as warm as it had. As though that look from the doorway had chilled it.

She shivered, said, "Come on, let's get back to the others."

The party was in the homestretch now, and they were dancing, he and she. Those little sketchy turns and fake half steps that are just an excuse to cover up a private conversation.

He said, "Well, let's take the apartment on Eighty-fourth Street, then. After all, if he'll give it to us for five dollars less a month like he said. . . . And with the furniture they're going to give us, we can fix it up to look like something——"

She said, "That girl in black can't take her eyes off you. Every time I look over there she's staring at you for all she's worth. If it was any night but tonight, I might begin to get worried."

He turned his head. "She isn't looking at me."

"She was until I called your attention to it."

"Who is she, anyway?"

She shrugged. "I thought all along she came with Fred Sterling and his bunch. You know how he always shows up anywhere with a whole posse. But he left quite some time ago and now I see she's still here. Maybe she decided to stay on alone. Whoever she is, I like the way she handles herself. None of this cheap dazzle stuff. I've been watching, she's had her troubles all evening long, poor thing. Every time she tries to sneak out on the terrace alone, three or four of the men mistake it for a come-on and make a beeline after her, then a minute later she'll come in again, usually by the side door, still alone. What she does to get rid of them that fast I don't know, but she must have it down to a science. They'll come slinking in again themselves right afterward, one by one, with that foolish look men have when they've been stymied. It's a regular sideshow."

She touched her hand lightly to his lapel as a signal; they stopped on the half turn.

"Some more people are leaving; I'll have to see them off. Be right back, darling. Miss me while I'm gone."

He watched her go, standing there like a flagpole on which the flag has suddenly been run down. When the light blue gown had whisked from sight at one end of the room, he turned and went out the other way, onto the terrace for a breath of air. He felt a little sticky under the collar; dancing always made him warm, anyway.

The lights of the city streaked off below him like the luminous spokes of a warped wheel. An indistinctly outlined, pearly moon seemed to drip down the sky like a clot of incandescent tapioca thrown up against the night by a cosmic comic. He lit the after-the-dance, while-waiting-for-her-to-come-back cigarette. He felt good, looking down at the town that had nearly had him licked once. "I'm all set now," he thought. "I'm young. I've got love, I've got a clear track. The rest is a cinch."

The terrace ran along the entire front of the apartment. At one end it made a turn around to the side of the penthouse superstructure, and the moon couldn't follow it. It was dark there.

There were no floor-length windows, either, just an infrequently used side door whose solid composition blacked out light.

He drifted around the turn, because there was another couple on the other way and he didn't want to crowd them. He stood in the exact right angle formed by the two directions of the ledge, and now he had two views instead of one.

And then suddenly—she must have slipped unnoticed out through the side door and come along from that direction toward him—that ubiquitous girl in black was standing there a foot or two away from him, looking out into the distance, the same way he was. She was weirdly like a white marble bust floating in the air without any pedestal, for the black of her dress was swallowed up in the blackness of the trough they both stood in.

"Swell, isn't it?" he suggested. After all, they were at the same party together.

She didn't seem to want to talk about that, so maybe it wasn't so swell to her.

At that instant Corey came along, conquest bound. He'd evidently had his eye on her for some time past, but the wheel of opportunity had only now spun his way. Bliss's presence didn't deter him in the least. "You go inside," he ordered arbitrarily. "'Don't be a hog, you're engaged."

The girl said in quick interruption, "Do you want to be a dear?"

"Sure I want to be a dear."

"Then get me a big tinkly highball."

He thumbed Bliss. "He does that better than I do."

"It would taste better coming from you." It was primitive, but it worked. Corey came back with it. She accepted it from him, held it out above the coping, slowly tilted it until the glass was bottom up and empty. Then she gravely handed it back. "Now go in and get me another."

Corey got the point. It would have been hard to miss it. The suave man-about-town glaze shattered momentarily and one of those aforementioned glimpses of jungle showed through the rent. Not travelogue jungle, either. A flash of white coursed over his face, lingering longest around his mouth in a sort of blood-less pucker. He stepped in and went for her neck with both hands, in businesslike silence.

"Whoa—easy," Bliss moved quickly, blocked them off before they could get to her, deflected them up into the air. By the time they came down again, Corey already had them under control. He bunched them in his pockets, perhaps to make sure of keep-ing them that way. Vocal resentment came belatedly, after the physical had already been reined in.

"Any twist that thinks she can make a monkey outta me . . . !" He turned around and strode back from where he'd come.

Bliss turned to follow. After all, what was she to him?

Her hand flashed out, pinned him at her side. "Don't go. I want to talk to you." It dropped away again as soon as she saw that she had gained her point.

He waited, listening.

"You don't know me, do you?"

"I've been trying to find out who you are all evening." He hadn't; he'd paid her less attention than any man there. It was the gallant thing to say, that was all.

"You saw me once before, but you don't remember. But I do. You were in a car with four others——"

"I've been in a car with four others lots of times, so many times I really can't——"

"Its license number was D3827."

"I've got a rotten head for figures."

"It was kept in a garage up on Exterior Avenue in the Bronx. And it was never called for afterward. Isn't that strange? It must still be there, rusted away . . ."

"I don't remember any of that," he said, baffled. "But say, who are you, anyway? There's something electrifying about you——"

"Too much can cause a short circuit." She moved a step or two away as though she had lost interest in him as unaccountably as she had developed it. She lifted the jet-spangled scarf from her head, held it spun out in a straight line before, her hands far apart, let the breeze flutter it forward.

Suddenly she gave a little exclamation. It was gone. Her hands still measured off its length. An aerial wire, invisible against the night, came down diagonally right there where she was, riveted to the facade below the ledge by a little porcelain insulation knob. She flashed him a look of half-comic surprise, then bent over, peering down.

"There it is, right there! It's caught on that little round white thing. . . ."

She plunged one arm down, probing into space. A moment later she had straightened again with a frustrated smile. "It's just an inch away from my fingers. Maybe you'd have better luck; you probably have a longer reach."

He got up on the coping, squatting on both heels. He cupped one hand to its inner edge, as a brake to keep from going over too far. His head turned away from her, searching for it.

She stepped forward behind him, palms out-turned as if in sanctimonious negation, then recoiled again as quickly. The slight impact forced a hissing breath from her, a sound that was explanation, malediction and expiation all in one.

"Mrs. Nick Killeen!"

He must have heard it. It must have been a spark in his darkening mind for a moment that went out as he went out.

The ledge was empty. She and the night had it to themselves. Through the terrace windows, around the turn, the radio was pulsing to a rumba and voices were laughing. One, louder than the others, exclaimed, "Keep it up, you've got it now!"

Marjorie accosted her on her way in a moment later. "I'm looking for my fiancé." She used the word with proud possessiveness, touching her ring with unconscious ostentation as she did so. "Is he out there, do you know?"

The girl in black smiled courteously. "He was, the last time I saw him." She moved on down the long room, briskly yet not too hurriedly, drawing more than one pair of admiring masculine eyes after her as she went.

The maid and butler were no longer on duty in the cloakroom adjoining the front door, came back only as they were summoned. Just as the front door was closing unobtrusively, without their having been disturbed, the house telephone connected with the downstairs entrance began to ring. It went on unanswered for a few moments.

Marjorie came inside again from the terrace, remarking to those nearest her, "That's strange. He doesn't seem to be out there."

Her mother, who had finally been compelled to attend to the neglected telephone in person, screamed harrowingly from somewhere out near the entrance, just once. The party had come to an end.

III

Postmortem on Bliss

LEW WANGER LEFT the cab with its door teetering open and elbowed his way through the small knot of muted onlookers who had collected about it. "What is it?" he asked the cop, showing him something from a vest pocket.

"Cash in." The patrolman pointed almost vertically. "From up there to down here."

Somebody's midnight edition of tomorrow morning's paper had been requisitioned, expanded with its component leaves spread end to end and formed into a mound along the ground. One foot, in a patent-leather evening oxford, stuck out at one corner.

"I understand they're having a blowout up there. Probably had a drink too many, leaned too far over and lost his balance." He tipped a section of the news sheet back, for Wanger's benefit.

One of the spectators, who hadn't been expecting this and was standing too close, turned his head aside, cupped a precautionary hand to his mouth and backed out in a hurry.

"Well, what'd y'expect, violets?" the cop called after him antagonistically.

Wanger squatted down on his heels and began to knead at a rigidly contracted fist that was showing at the upper right-hand corner of the mound. He finally extracted what looked like a swirl of frozen black smoke.

"Dame's handkerchief," supplied the cop.

"Scarf," corrected Wanger. "Too big for a handkerchief." He looked down again at the shrouded body.

"I know him by sight," the night doorman of the building supplied. "I think they were announcing his engagement to their daughter tonight, up at the Elliotts'. That's the penthouse."

"Well, I'd better get up there and get it over with," Wanger sighed. "Just routine; probably won't take more than ten or fifteen minutes at the most."

At daybreak he was still hammering at the disheveled, exhausted guests ranged before him. "And do you mean to say there's not one of you here even knew this girl's name or had never seen her before tonight?" All heads kept shaking dully.

"Didn't anyone ask her name? What kind of people are you, anyway?"

"We all did at one time or another," a dejected man said. "She wouldn't give it. Passed it off each time with some crack like 'What's in a name?'"

"Okay, then she was a gate-crasher, pure and simple. Now what I want to find out is why, what her motive was." Marjorie's mother came back into the room at this point, and he turned to her. "How about it, any valuables missing, anything stolen from the apartment?"

"No," she sobbed, "not a thing's been touched. I just got through checking up."

"Then robbery wasn't the motive for the intrusion. She seems to have avoided and discouraged all the rest of you young fellows all evening long, according to what you say; singled Bliss out as soon as there was a chance of getting him alone. Yet according to what *you* say—" he turned to Corey "—he didn't seem to recognize her from the description passed on to him by the doorman at his own flat. And when he arrived here and finally saw her, he acted as though she was a perfect stranger to him. That is, assuming it was the same girl.

"That's about all there is to be done up here for the present. Has anyone anything to add to this description you've given me of her?"

No one had; she had been seen by so many people, it was exhaustive in itself. As the guests filed mournfully out one by one, giving their names and addresses in case they should be wanted for further questioning, Corey edged up to Wanger. He was full of drink and cold sober at the same time. "I was his best friend," he said huskily. "How do you see it? What do you figure it for?"

"Well, I'll tell you," Wanger answered as he prepared to leave, "not that you're entitled to be taken into my confidence any more than anyone else. There isn't anything to show that it wasn't an accident—but one thing. The fact that she cleared out of here so fast right after it happened, instead of staying to face the music like all the rest of you. Another very incriminating piece of behavior is that when she met Miss Elliott in the doorway and the latter asked her if she'd seen him, she calmly answered that he was out there, instead of screaming blue murder that he'd just gone over, which was the normal thing to do. There's always a possibility, of course, that he didn't go over until after she'd already left him and gone inside. But what argues against that is that he took that black scarf of hers down with him. That makes it look very much as though she was still with him at the actual instant it happened. Yet she could have dropped it or even given it to him to hold for her, then gone in.

"You see, the thing is fifty-fifty so far; everything you can bring to bear on one side balances nicely with something you can bring to bear on the other. What'll finally tip the scales one way or the other, as far as I'm concerned, is her ultimate behavior. If she comes forward within a day or two to identify or clear herself, as soon as she hears we're looking for her, the chances are it'll turn out to have been an accident and she ran out simply to escape the notoriety, knowing she had no right up here. If she remains hidden and we have to go out hunting for her, I think we can say murder and not be very far from right."

He pocketed the description and other data he'd taken down. "We'll get her, either way, don't worry."

But they didn't.

Evening accessories department, Bonwit Teller department store, fifteen days later:

"Yes, this is our twelve-dollar wimple. The only place it could have been purchased is here; it's a special with us."

"All right, now call your sales staff in here. I want to find out if any of them remembers selling one to a woman whose description follows. . . ."

And when they'd assembled and he'd repeated it three times over, a mousy little person with glasses stepped forward. "I—I remember selling one of these numbers in black, to a beautiful girl answering that description, a little over two weeks ago."

"Good! Dig up the sales slip. I want the address it was sent to."

Fifteen minutes later: "The customer paid cash and took it with her; no name or address was given."

"Is that the customary way you make these sales?"

"No, they're a luxury item; they're usually delivered. In this case it was at the customer's special request that she took it right along with her, I remember that."

Wanger (under his breath): "To cover her tracks."

Wanger's report to his superior, three weeks later:

". . . And not a trace of her since. Not a sign to show who she was, where she came from, where she went. Nor why she did it— *if* she did it. I've investigated Bliss's past exhaustively, checked back almost to the first girl he ever kissed, and she doesn't appear anywhere in it. The testimony of the doorman at his flat, and of his friend Corey, seems to show that he did *not* know this girl, whoever she was. Yet she deliberately discouraged and shunned everyone else at this party, until she had maneuvered to get him alone out on that terrace. So mistaken identity won't jibe, either.

"In short, the only indication it was not an accident is the strange behavior of this mystery woman and her subsequent disappearance and refusal to come forward and clear up the matter. On the other hand, other than the above, there is no positive indication it was murder, either."

Wanger's record on Ken Bliss:

Met death in fall from seventeenth-floor terrace, 4:30 A.M., May 20. Last seen with woman about twenty-six, fair skin,

yellow hair, blue eyes, five feet five inches. Identity unknown. *Wanted for questioning.*

Motive: Uncertain if crime was committed, but, if so, probably passional or jealousy. No record of former relationship.

Witnesses: None.

Evidence: Black evening scarf, purchased Bonwit Teller's,
May 19.

Case Unsolved.

PART TWO

MITCHELL

He starts as one who, hearing a deer's tread,
Beholds a panther stealing forth instead.

—DE MAUPASSANT

I

The Woman

MIRIAM—LAST NAME LONG forgotten within the confines of the Helena Hotel—was a short pugnacious person the color of old leather. She had three things she clung to tenaciously; her British citizenship—which had been passively acquired through the accident of birth on the island of Jamaica; a pair of gold-coin earrings; and her "system" of doing rooms. No one had ever made the slightest attempt to interfere with the first two, and the few abortive efforts at tampering with the latter had met with resounding failure.

Numerical progression of the rooms had nothing to do with it. Nor had their location along the dim, creaky, varileveled corridors. In fact, it was a sort of mystic algebra known only to the innermost workings of her mind. No one could disturb it—not with impunity, anyway. Not without bringing on a long malevolent tirade, down endless reaches of labyrinthine corridor, that went on—or seemed to—for hours afterward, long after the original cause of it had slunk away, frustrated.

"The fo'teen come after the seventeen. It got to wait tell I finish the seventeen. I ain't never yet do fo'teen first."

Nor did this precedence have anything to do with gratuities, which were in any case an almost nonexistent factor at the Helena. Habit, perhaps, would be the closest guess to what after all was a purely emotional state of mind on Miriam's part.

The wheel of the "system" having finally, at the appointed hour and fraction thereof of the day, swung around to "the nineteen," Miriam advanced down a particularly moldering length of corridor far toward the back, tin bucket in one hand, long pole in the other, at the working end of which could still be detected stray wisps of fibrous fuzz.

She halted before "the nineteen," reversed her key and sounded it twice against the woodwork. This was a mere formality, since she would have been as highly outraged at finding "the nineteen" in as at having her "system" interfered with. "The nineteen" had never been in at this hour yet. "The nineteen" had no right to be in at this hour.

Nor was the formality of the key tap due to scrupulous observance of hotel regulations, either. It was reflex action. She could no longer enter a door without doing it. Inevitably, on returning home to her own furnished room at the end of the day, she gave that same trip-hammer tap on the panel before inserting her own private key into the lock.

She threw open the door challengingly and advanced into a small and singularly unprepossessing room. The pattern of the carpet had been ground into oblivion. A sort of gray green fungus was all that now covered the floorboards. A whitewashed-brick wall blocked the eye a few feet outside the window. Through this a shaft of sunlight struggled downward at an angle that was enough to break its back. The room would have been better off without it, if only to preserve an illusion of cleanliness, for it was fuming like a Seidlitz powder with masses of dust particles.

On the wall above the bed was ranged an array of girls' photographs of varying sizes, all mounted, framed and glassed over. Miriam did not even deign to raise her eyes to these. Most of them had been up for years. The one "nineteen" was going with now would never get up there, she opined, because she couldn't afford to have a picture taken and he couldn't afford to have it mounted, framed and glassed over. And there wasn't any more room left on that side, anyway. He was too old now to begin a new side. And if he wasn't, he ought to be. Which disposed of that matter.

The bed made, with frenziedly swirling effects on the dust motes in the sunbeam, Miriam narrowed the room door considerably but without closing it altogether. There was nothing furtive about the way she did this; there was rather an injured defiance. She even put this into words, aloud, it was felt so keenly. "Hidin' it all the time. Always hidin' it. Who he think going to take it anyway? Who he think want it?"

She gave her mouth a preparatory drying—or perhaps it was a whetting—along the back of her hand. She opened the closet door, stooped, disrupted a cairn of soiled shirts on the floor in one corner of it, brought up a bottle of gin like someone lifting a rabbit out of a hole.

She displayed no satisfaction at the sight of it, only moral indignation. "Who he think come in here, anyway, but me? He know ain't nobody come in here but me! Suspicionin' people that way!"

She tilted the bottle, lowered it again. Then she came out with it, advanced to the washbasin, turned on the cold-water tap. With a dexterity that bespoke long practice she switched the open bottle mouth under it and out again, just enough to restore the contents to their former level, no more. This was not so difficult as it appeared. There were mistrustful pencil gauge marks plainly visible on two of the four corners of the frosted glass to guide her. She corrected a slight discrepancy she had been guilty of in favor of the bottle, by means of her mouth. She was heaving with a sense almost of persecution by now. "Ol' miser! Stingy ol' thing!" she glowered with Antillean passion and a slight accompanying tinkle from the gold-coin earrings. "One thing I don't like is people mistrustin' me!"

She returned the bottle to its bourn, closed the closet, restored the room door to its former width and entered upon the second stage of her duties, which consisted in thrusting the staff with the errant fuzz at random places along the base of the walls, like someone spearing salmon from a rock in midstream.

It was while she was engaged in this slightly puzzling maneuver that she became aware of being observed. She turned her head and there was a lady standing out there in the hallway, looking through the open doorway. Miriam knew at a single glance that she did not live in the hotel, and she rose accordingly in Miriam's esteem. Her low regard for and truculence toward those who did was matched only by her high regard for and willingness to be affable to those who didn't. A blanket order, both ways.

"Yes, ma'am?" she said with cordial interest. "You lookin' for Mist' Mitchell?"

The lady was so friendly and so soft-spoken. "No," she smiled. "I just happened to drop in to see a friend of mine, and she's not in. I was on my way back to the elevator, and I'm afraid I became a little confused. . . ."

Miriam rested on her mop handle like a Venetian gondolier at ease and hoped the lady wouldn't go right away.

She didn't. She advanced an unnoticeable step nearer the threshold but still remained well outside the confines of the room proper. She gave the impression of an overpowering interest in Miriam and her conversation.

Miriam visibly preened herself standing there in the sulfurous sun shaft, wriggled almost ecstatically around the mop pole.

"You know," the lady confided with an enchanting woman-to-woman intimacy of manner, "I always think you can tell so much about a person just by looking at the room they live in,"

"Yes, indeed, you sho' right about that," Miriam agreed heartily.

"Just take this one here—as long as you happen to be in it tidying it up and I happen to be on my way past the door. Now, I don't know a thing about the person living in it——"

"Mist' Mitchell?" prompted Miriam, almost mesmerically engrossed by now. Her chin had come to rest on the rounded point of the mop handle.

The lady made a careless gesture of one hand. "Mitchell or whatever the name may be—I don't know him and I've never seen him. But just let me tell you what his room shows me—and you correct me if I'm wrong."

Miriam squirmed her shoulders with anticipatory delight. "Go 'head." she encouraged breathlessly. This was nearly as exciting as having your palm read by a fortune-teller, free of charge.

"He's not very tidy. That necktie twisted around the light fixture——"

"He's a slob," confirmed Miriam pugnaciously.

"He's not very well off. But of course the hotel itself would tell me that; it's not very expensive——"

"He's been a month and a half behind in his rent fo' eight years straight!" divulged Miriam darkly.

The lady paused—not like one who is trying to put one over on you, but like one who wants to weigh her words carefully before committing herself. "He doesn't work," she said finally. "There's an early edition of today's paper standing on end in the wastebasket. I can see it from here. He evidently gets up around noon, reads for a while before going out for the rest of the day."

Miriam nodded enthralled, unable to take her eyes off this apparition of wit, wisdom and graciousness. The mop handle could have been snatched away from under her and she probably would have retained her half-inclined position unaltered, without noticing it. "He shiftless, all right. He live on some kine of a sojer pension come in each month, I dunno what it is." She shook her head reverently. "Gee, you sho' good."

"He's lonely, hasn't many friends." Her eyes went up to the wall. "All those pictures up there, they're a sign of loneliness, not popularity. If he had many friends, he wouldn't have to bother with pictures."

Miriam had never thought of it in this light before. In fact, if the pictures had meant anything at all to her—which they hadn't for years past now—they had stood for a certain nastiness of mind on their owner's part, a gloating over his misdeeds. In the beginning she had even expressed this aloud once or twice, at sight of them. To wit: "Dirty ol' thing!"

"Even," the lady went on, "if he actually knew all those girls well— which he probably didn't—he knew them only one at a time, not all in a group. There are the ear puffs of right after the war and the Japanese-doll bob of the early twenties and the flat, shoulder-length hair of a few years ago. . . ."

Miriam had swiveled her head, was looking around and up at the wall behind her; the rounded point of the mop handle now rested just above one ear. She even scratched her head by moving it slightly back and forth in this position.

"He's never actually found the girl he's looking for; there wouldn't be so many of them up there if he had. There wouldn't be any of them up there if he had. But they . . ." She tapped the rim of one of her lower teeth reflectively. "Blend them all together, into one composite picture, and they try to tell you what he has been looking for."

"Blame!" marveled Miriam, who apparently hadn't even known he had been looking for anything. Or at least, not something that you discussed in polite company.

"He's been looking for mystery. An illusion. A type of girl who is not to be found anywhere in this world. Who does not exist outside his own imagination. A rootless creature floating detachedly above the everyday world, with no points of contact. An odalisque. A Mata Hari."

"Who?" queried Miriam alertly, swinging her head around.

"Just look at them up there. Not one of them as she really is—or was, rather. Soft-focused in tulle, haloed in photographic mist, peering through a lace fan, ogling the camera in reverse through a mirror, biting a rose. . . ."

She smiled a little, not altogether unkindly. "A man and his dreams."

"I 'spect he never goin' get one like he really wants her," suggested Miriam.

"You never can tell," the lady in the doorway smiled. "You never can tell."

Then she deferred to Miriam with an enchanting, quizzical little quirk of her head. "Tell the truth now, haven't I been right more than I've been wrong?"

"You been right all the way!" Miriam championed her stoutly.

"You see? That's what I mean. It just goes to show you what an empty room can tell you."

"Don' it though! It sho' do."

"Well, I mustn't keep you from your work any longer." She gave a chummy little flurry of her fingers, an extra-warm smile of parting, and moved on her way.

Miriam sighed regretfully as the doorway showed blank. She let the mop staff stagger against the wall, went over to the entry and stood in it, watching her down the hall and around the turn. Then that showed blank, too.

She sighed again, more disconsolately than ever. What an enjoyable conversation! What an instructive, entertaining one! What a shame it had to be over so soon, couldn't have kept on a little longer! Just until she finished one more room, for instance.

The elevator door clashed faintly, out of sight around the turn there, and she was gone for good now. Miriam moved unwillingly back into the room to her uncompleted task.

"She sho' was nice," she murmured wistfully. "I bet she don' ever come back again, either."

II

Mitchell

MITCHELL CAME INTO the shabby lobby of his hotel at his usual time, folded paper under his arm. He stopped at the desk to see if there was any mail. He got that special look from the clerk, reserved for those who are chronically a month and a half behind in their room rent. He got three letters.

The first was a note from Maybelle, his blond friend from the restaurant. The second was a mistake, belonged in the pigeonhole above. The third one was either a circular or a bill, he could tell right away by looking at it. The address was typed, and the envelope bore no return address. He didn't open it right away, for that reason. He could scent bills and advertisements a mile away.

He went upstairs, closed the door and looked around the room. He'd been living here twelve years. The room had acquired facets of his personality in that time. There were framed photographs of girls galore all over the walls. A regular gallery. It wasn't that he was a roué; he was a romanticist. He'd kept looking for his ideal. He'd wanted her to be glamorous, mysterious. Masks and fans and secret rendezvouses and that sort of stuff. And all he'd ever got was waitresses from Childs and salesgirls from Hearn's. Pretty soon it would be too late to find Her anymore; pretty soon it wouldn't matter.

He hung up his coat, with the third letter making a white scar above its side pocket. He got out the gin bottle from underneath his dirty shirts on the floor at the back of the closet, where the maid couldn't get at it. He allowed himself only two fingers every evening, parceled out each bottle so that it lasted two weeks. He shot the pickup bodily into the back of his mouth, without putting lips to the jigger glass at all.

Here it was night again, and nothing wonderful, nothing glamorous was ever going to happen to him. Just cheapness. A cheap hotel room, a cheap man in his shirt sleeves, cheap gin, cheap regrets. He supposed he might as well call up Maybelle now as later and get it over with. He knew he was going to in the end, anyway. It was a case of Maybelle or nothing. But he knew just what she'd say, just what she'd wear, just what she'd think. Beer and liverwurst.

He picked up the phone and gave the number of her rooming house. Then he always had to wait while her landlady yelled all the way up the stairwell to the fourth floor for her to come down. He'd done it so often he knew just how long to allow for it. He left the phone and went over to his coat to get out a cigarette. He saw that third, unopened envelope in his side pocket. He pulled it out, tore it open.

A crimson ticket fell out. There was nothing else in the envelope. "Elgin Theater. Loge A-1. Good only Tuesday evening." That was tonight. "$3.30," it said in the corner. It couldn't be *good;* it must be some kind of dummy. He turned it over and over and over, but there was no catch on it anywhere, no additional payment to be made. It was authentic. Who had sent him such a thing?

The phone was making rasping metallic noises. He went back to it. "She'll be right down," Maybelle's landlady was saying, against background noises of clump, clump, clump. She always came down with her shoes left open and flapping.

"Sorry," he said firmly, "I got the wrong number," and hung up.

He started to get ready. It rang back when he was at the hair-smoothing stage. It was Maybelle. "Mitch, was that you just called me here?"

"No," he lied remorselessly.

"Well, am I gonna see you tonight?"

"Gee, no," he whined falsely. "I'm laid up in bed with a touch of grippe."

"Well, should I stop over and keep you company?"

"No, don't do that," he said hastily. "You might catch it from me and lose a week's wages." He hung up before she could bedevil him with any further unwanted kindnesses.

He was almost sure, when he got down to the Elgin and presented it at the door, that the ticket chopper was going to turn him down. Instead, he accepted it, even passed him in with an extra touch of deference because it was a loge seat.

Then it was *good*, there could be no further doubt of it. But who had sent it to him? Would the person be up there in the loge when he got there? Suppose there was more than one; how would he know which one it was?

There wasn't anybody in the loge at all, he discovered to his secret disappointment when the usher had led him to it. Each loge was fitted with four chairs, walled off from its neighbors on either side and from the balcony behind it. There was more privacy to be obtained in them than in any other part of the house, even the boxes.

He felt funny sitting there alone with the three vacant chairs around him, kept looking around to see if anyone was coming. Even kept half expecting to be tapped on the shoulder by the usher and told a mistake had been made and he'd have to leave, there was someone else downstairs at the box office claiming his ticket. But nothing like that happened. All the other loges gradually filled up, but no one came near this center one, which was the choicest of the lot. At overture time, when the house lights went down and plunged the audience into blue twilight, its three remaining chairs were still unspoken for, almost as though they had been bought up ahead of time to make sure they would remain unoccupied.

The play began, and as its glamour and make-believe unfolded before him, little by little he began to forget the strange circumstances that had brought him here, to lose himself in its spell. Then suddenly—at exactly what point during the first act she'd arrived he did not know—there was someone already sitting there next to him. There hadn't even been a flick of the usher's flashlight or a rustle of garments to warn him. Or if there had, he'd missed them.

No one ever came to claim those two other chairs just in back of them. He never saw any more of the show than just that first half of the first act. He couldn't take his eyes off her from then on. She was beautiful; gee, she was beautiful! She was red haired and had a face like a cameo. She had a dark velvet wrap around her, lighter on the inside, and she seemed to rise out of its folds like a—like a nymph out of a seashell.

He would never have dared to speak to her, but suddenly she had turned to him, was holding a cigarette to her lips, waiting for a light. "Would you mind?" she said, with just a trace of foreign accent. "One is allowed to smoke in these loges, I believe."

And that was the start of the acquaintanceship.

He had everything in readiness long before she could be expected to come. He still couldn't believe she'd meant it, that she was really coming here to see him. It had been her own suggestion, he would never have dreamed of. . . . He had told her how to reach the room without having to pass through the inquisitive lobby downstairs, by the service stairs at the back of the house that only old-timers like him knew about. And yet, with all that, she had managed to convey, tactfully and deftly, that this wasn't to be an affair. Certainly it wasn't; you don't have an affair with your ideal. You worship her.

He stood back, looking the place over for the tenth time. All those girls' pictures that he'd taken down from the walls had left yellowed stains behind them from being up so long. What did he want those counterfeits for, now that he'd found the real thing at last? He'd got hold of a screen and put it around the bed. He couldn't do much else for the room; it still remained a shabby $8-a-week cubbyhole.

He rubbed his hands nervously. He looked in the mirror again to see how the new necktie looked on him.

The phone rang, and he almost tripped all over himself trying to get to it fast enough. Wasn't she coming? Had she changed her mind? Then he slumped disappointedly, with a wearied grimace. It was only Maybelle.

"How's your grippe? I been worried about you all day, Mitch. Look, I snitched some of the rest'runt's chicken broth that goes with our special dolla' dinna', I'm gonna bring it over in a container, it's the best thing for you when you're laid up like that."

He writhed agonizedly. God, tonight of all nights! "I thought you had the night shift Wednesday nights," he snarled ungraciously.

"I changed places with one of the other girls so I could come over and take care of you."

"No, some other time, I can't see you tonight——"

She was starting to snivel at the other end of the line. "All right for you! You'll be sorry!"

He hung up heartlessly just as the delicate tap he'd been waiting to hear sounded on the room door.

He opened the door and Romance came in, just as he'd always daydreamed it would, someday, somewhere. She was muffled in that same velvet cape she'd worn at the theater.

He didn't know what to say or how to act; he'd never been with an Ideal before. "Did you find those stairs all right? I— maybe I should have gone down and met you at the corner."

He turned on the radio, but it was a sports commentary, so he turned it right off again.

She brought a bottle of something out from under the folds of her cape. Yet she could even make that act, which would have seemed unspeakably shoddy if committed by anyone like Maybelle, appear gracious and intriguing. "This is for us," she said. "Arak, I brought it as my contribution to our evening." It hadn't been opened yet, foil still sealed its neck, and he had to pull up the cork with a screw.

It was heady stuff, but it made you see the world through

rose-colored glasses. It took away his tongue-tiedness, made him speak without difficulty and say the things that came to his mind. "You're just like I always dreamed of someone being, almost as though you came out of my own head."

"The really clever woman is all things to all men. Like the chameleon, she takes her coloring from his ideal of her. It is her job to find out what that is. Those pictures on the wall, they told so plainly what you had looked for in women——"

He nearly dropped the glass he was holding, stared at her wide-eyed. "How did you know there were pictures on the wall? Have you ever been in this room before?"

She drank a sip of liquor, coughed very slightly. "No," she said. "But it is easy to see from the stains that there were pictures there. And anyone who does that is a romantic and romanticizes women."

"Oh," he said, and took up his glass again. His perceptions were already a little dulled. He was too happy to be captious. "It's funny. . . ."

"What is?"

"Just by being here, you change this mangy room into something warm and glamourous. You take away twenty years and make me feel—like I useta feel walking down the bullyvards on leave under a tin hat, and around every corner I was sure I'd find. . . ."

"What?"

"I don't know, something wonderful. I never did, but it didn't matter, because there was always another corner. It was the feeling that mattered. It made your footsteps sing. I've always wanted it back again, but I was never able to get it anymore after that. You must be magic."

"Black or white?"

He smiled vacantly. He evidently didn't get the allusion.

"I'll have to go now." She stood up, crossed over to the dresser. "One more drink before I do. I think there's enough in it for one more." She held up the bottle eyed it against the light. They had been using the bureau top for a serving table. She filled the two glasses, then interrupted herself, letting them stand there on it a moment, a considerable distance apart. "I must make myself beautiful—for your last look at me," she smiled across her shoulder.

A little metal powder holder flashed open in her hand. She leaned across the bureau top toward the mirror. She made little flurried motions that bespoke the will rather than the deed, for the vast majority of them failed to come anywhere near the surface of her nose. She was really powdering the air between it and the mirror.

He sat there, smiling over at her in hazy benevolence.

Her nose didn't grow any noticeably whiter—but then maybe that was the whole art of powdering it, so that it wouldn't show. A grain or two of white had fallen on the dark-wood surface of the dresser. She bent down toward them, the epitome of neatness. Her breath stirred them off into oblivion.

She picked up the glasses and went back to him.

He looked up at her with an almost doglike devotion. "I can't believe all this is really happening to me. That you're really here. That you're bending over me like this, handing me a glass. That your breath is stirring my hair. That there's just a little sweetness, like one carnation in a whole room, in the air around me. . . ."

He'd put his glass down meanwhile, and so had she, as if in some kind of obligatory accompaniment.

"When you go outside the door, I'll know it wasn't true. I'll dream about you tonight, and in the morning I won't know which was the dream and which was the real part. I don't already."

"Drink." And then as he reached for the wrong one, "No, that one's yours, over there. Are you forgetting?" she said with unexpected sharpness.

"To what?"

"To the coming dream. May it be a long and pleasant one."

He hitched his glass. "To the coming dream."

She eyed it as he set it down again half-drained. "This isn't our first meeting," she remarked thoughtfully.

"No, last night at the theater——"

"Not there, either. You saw me once before. On the steps of a church. Do you remember?"

"On the steps of a church?" His head lolled idiotically; he straightened it with an effort. "What were you doing there?"

"Getting married. Now do you remember?"

Absently, absorbed in what she was saying, he finished what was in his glass. "Was I at the wedding?"

"Ah, yes, you were at the wedding—very much so." She got up abruptly, snapped the switch of the midget radio. "We'll have a little music at this point."

A guttural, malevolent trombone seemed to snarl into the air about them. She began to pivot about him, turning faster and faster, skirt expanding about her knees.

Nobody's sweetheart now.
And it all seems wrong somehow——

He backed his hand to his forehead. "I can't see you so clearly—what's happening—are the lights flickering?"

Faster and faster went the solo dance, the dance of triumph and obsequy. "The lights are still, it's you that is flickering."

His glass fell, crashed on the floor. He started to writhe, clutch at himself. "My chest—it's being torn apart. Get help, a doctor——"

"No doctor could reach here in time." She was like a spinning top now, seeming to recede down the long vista of the walls. His dimming eyes could see her as a blur of brightness; then, like white metal cooling, little by little she seemed to go out forever in the dark.

He was on the floor now at her feet, moaning out along the carpet in a foaming expiration; ". . . only wanted to make you happy. . . ."

From far away a voice whispered mockingly, "You have . . . you have . . ." Then trailed off into silence.

She backed the room door after her, about to close it inextricably into the frame, then froze to statuesque stillness, holding it ajar that fraction of an inch that meant reentry could be gained at her volition.

They looked at each other, a foot apart. Maybelle was blond and buxom and blowsy, and holding a cylinder of some sort done up untidily in brown paper. The woman in the velvet cape, flung around her in a sort of jaunty defiance that somehow suggested a toreador, eyed her calculatingly, watchfully.

The other spoke first, pouting with overreddened, full-blown lips. "I brought this over to Mitch. If he doesn't want to see me, he doesn't have to; I understand now. But tell him-"

"Yes?"

"Tell him I said he should drink it while it's still hot."

The woman in the cape glanced over her shoulder at the hairbreadth crack of door, too narrow to permit vision. "They saw you come in just now, downstairs?"

"Yes, sure."

"They saw you carrying that soup?"

"Yes, sure."

How easy to have inveigled her into the room. She had moved the screen out and around his body, concealing it, when the first warning knock at the door had come. How easy, in the moment or two before this stupid heifer discovered him, to have silenced her forever, with the same glass he had just drunk from. Or to have left her there, involved, too stupid ever to clear herself.

She turned back to her. The door clicked definitely shut behind her. "Get down there where you come from, get away from here fast." It wasn't said in menace, but in whispered warning.

Maybelle just opened China-blue eyes and stared at her stupidly. "Quick! Every minute that you spend up here alone will count against you. Be sure you take that container down with you again, unopened. Let them know you couldn't get in—gather people around you, protect yourself!" She gave the slow-thinking lummox a push that started her involuntarily down the corridor toward the front of the building. From the turn at the end of it the blonde looked back dazedly. "But wha-what's wrong? What happened?"

"Your friend is dead in there and I killed him. I'm only trying to save you from becoming involved yourself, you fool. I have nothing against—other women."

But Maybelle hadn't waited to hear the last. She emitted a

series of noises like a nail scratching glass, fled from view with a great surging wallow.

The woman in the velvet cape moved swiftly, but with a neat economy of movement that robbed her going of all semblance of flight, to the hinged service door at the other end of the corridor, giving onto the unguarded back stairs.

III

Postmortem on Mitchell

WANGER'S SUPERIOR DIDN'T put him on it until nearly a week after it had happened. A man named Cleary had been working on it in the meantime and getting exactly nowhere.

"Say, listen, Wanger, there's a peculiar case over at the Helena Hotel. I've just been reading the reports sent in on it, and it occurred to me it has certain features in common with that Bliss incident—remember that, six months or so ago? At first glance they're not at all alike. There's no doubt about this one, it's an out-and-out murder. But what gave me the notion was they both feature a woman who seems to have gone up in smoke immediately afterward, for all the trace we've ever been able to find of her. Also a complete lack of discoverable motive. Neither of which is exactly usual in our line. That's why I thought it'd be a good idea to have Cleary run through it for you, give you his findings; you talk to some of the people he's lined up. You see, you're familiar with that Bliss affair, he's not; you're in a better position to judge. If you think you detect any connection, no matter how slight, let me know, I'll assign you to it full-time."

Cleary said, "Here's what I've gotten so far, after seven days on it. It all stacks up very nicely, but it has no meaning. It's as irrational as the act of a feminine homicidal maniac, but I have definite proof that she is nothing of the sort, as you'll be able to judge for yourself later, when you hear it. Now, he died from a pinch or two of cyanide potassium introduced into a glass of arak——"

"Yes, I read that in the examiner's report."

"Here are transcriptions of the witnesses' statements. You can read them over later; I'll give you the gist of them now, as I go along. First of all, I found a red theater-ticket stub—you know, the remainder that's returned to the customer to hold after it's chopped at the door—in the lining of one of his pockets. I traced it back and here's the story: two nights before his death a very beautiful red-haired woman stepped up to the box office at the Elgin Theater and said she wanted to buy an entire loge outright. The ticket seller asked her what night she wanted it for, and she said that didn't matter, any night. What did matter was that she wanted to be sure of getting the entire loge. That was unusual for two reasons: with most customers the date is the important thing; they take the best they can get on the particular date they want. Secondly, the number of seats didn't seem to concern her, either; she didn't ask whether she was getting three, four or five. All she wanted was the entire loge for her own. He gave her the four seats for the first night they were available, which happened to be the very next night. Naturally the incident impressed him.

"Two of them were never used. Mitchell was seen by the theater staff to show up alone on that particular night and turn in one ticket. The same woman who had originally bought them also showed up alone, but a considerable time later, long after the curtain had gone up."

"Only one person is in a position to state for a fact that she was the same woman who bought them," Wanger warned him.

"The ticket seller; and that's his affidavit you have under your thumb there. He'd shuttered his box office for the night and happened to be standing watching the show from the mezzanine stairs; she passed him on her way up—alone—and he recognized her beyond any possibility of doubt.

"Now we come to the important part of the whole thing. I've questioned the usher on loge duty. What he tells me convinces me they were utter strangers to each other. He paid particular attention to the act of seating her for several reasons. He has fewer people to seat than the orchestra or balcony ushers. She came in unusually late and so stood out. She was strikingly beautiful and came alone, which seemed to him to be unusual.

"He watched closely, if not altogether intentionally, for the above reasons, as she settled herself in her seat. Neither one turned to greet the other. Neither one spoke or even nodded. He remained within earshot long enough to be sure of that. He's positive; by everything he's ever learned in all his years of theater ushering, that they were complete strangers.

"And that cinches it, to my mind. If they hadn't been, Mitchell would have waited for her down in the lobby instead of going up ahead. Any man would have, even the crudest.

"It was only during the intermission that the usher noticed they'd begun to talk to each other. And then it was in that diffident way of two people who are just becoming acquainted."

"In other words, it was a pickup."

"If they were strangers, how'd she get his ticket to him? She bought them, he showed up with one of them."

"Anonymously, through the mail. I found the envelope, also, in one of the pockets. The ticket was a vivid crimson. There's a faint pinkish discoloration visible on the inside of the envelope; somebody with sweaty hands, either at the post office or downstairs at the hotel desk—or, maybe Mitchell himself—handled it, dampened the dye a little. This is it here.

"She was only seen one more time after that. Then she vanished completely. I haven't been able to get a line on her since then. The night of the murder she wasn't seen entering or leaving the hotel. However, that isn't quite as confounding as it sounds, because there's a service stairs at the back that leads directly out into an alley without passing the lobby. The alley door works on a spring lock, can't be opened from the outside, but it could very easily have been left ajar to admit her. These precautions must have been her own suggestion, since she evidently came prepared to kill Mitchell."

"Then who was it saw her that one more time you just mentioned, after the theater episode?"

"The girl he was keeping steady company with, a waitress named Maybelle Hodges. She called at the room within a few moments after the time established for his death by the medical examination. When she knocked on the door, this woman came out. She'd been in there."

"What did the woman say to her?"

"She admitted she'd killed him, and advised the girl to go downstairs again, get away before she became involved herself."

Wanger felt his chin dubiously. "Do you think that statement's trustworthy?"

"Yes, because the girl's description of the woman, both as to appearance and the clothes she was wearing, tallies completely with that given me by the theater staff, so you see she couldn't very well have made the story up. And this brings up a point I mentioned before. She's not a homicidal maniac by any means;

she had a beautiful opportunity to kill the Hodges girl then and there. All she had to do was admit her to the room—there was a screen around his body. She had plenty of time. Instead she warned the girl off, for the girl's own sake.

"There's the whole thing. More material than we need, in one way. But the keystone that would give it a meaning is missing; no motive."

"No conceivable motive, and they didn't know each other, and she vanishes as completely as a streak of lightning after it's struck once," Wanger summed up, baffled. "Well, he sent me over here to see if I could make anything out of it. I'm only sure of one thing: this case strings along with the Bliss one; it's an accurate copy."

Chambermaid, fourth floor, Helena Hotel:

"I never seen her before, so I knew for a fact she didn't live in the hotel. I thought maybe she was visitin' somebody. She was just passin' by the hall that day. This was about, um, two weeks before it happened. Maybe mo'. She stopped and looked in the open door while I'm cleanin' his room, I said, 'Yes'm, you lookin' for Mr. Mitchell?' She said, 'No, but I always think you can learn so much about a pusson's character and habits just by lookin' at their rooms.' She talk so polite and refine' it's a pleasure to hear her. She look at the girls' pictures he have all over the wall and she say, 'He likes women to be mysterious, I can tell by them. Not one is an honest everyday pitcher of how those girls really look. They all tryin' to look like somethin' else, for his sake. Bitin' roses and starin' through lace fans. If one of 'em gave him her pitcher like she really was, he most likely wouldn't put it up.'

"That's all. And then before I knowed it, she gone away again, and I never seen her no mo' after that."

Clerk at Globe Liquor Store:

"Yes, I remember selling this. A thing as unusual as arak we don't sell more than a bottle a year. No, it was not her suggestion. I happened to come across it on the shelf and I thought it would be a good opportunity to get it off our hands, as long as she'd asked for something unusual and at the same time potent. She said she was making a present of it to a friend, and the more exotic it was the better pleased he would be. I'd already shown her vodka and aquavit. She decided on arak. She admitted she'd never sampled any of it herself. One funny thing: on her way out she gave me a peculiar smile and said, 'I find myself doing so many things these days that I've never done before.'

"No, not at all nervous. As a matter of fact she deliberately stood aside and told me to go ahead and wait on a man who wanted a bottle of rye in a hurry, while she was making up her mind. She said she wanted to take her time making a selection."

Wanger's superior said a week later, "So you think the two cases are related in some way, do you?"

"I do."

"Well, in just what way?"

"Only in this way: the same unknown woman is involved in both."

"Oh, no, there's where you're wrong, it couldn't possibly be," his chief overrode him, semaphoring with both hands. "I'll admit I had some vague notion along those lines myself when I spoke to you last week. But that won't stand up, man, it won't wash at all! Since then I've had time to look over the composite description Cleary obtained of her and sent in. That knocks it completely on the head. Take the Bliss one out of the files a minute, bring it in here. Now just look at the two of them. Put them side by side a minute."

Bliss file	Mitchell file
yellow blond hair	red hair
five feet five	five feet seven
fresh complexion	sallow complexion
blue eyes	gray blue eyes
about twenty-six	about thirty-two
speech shows educa-tion and refinement	talks with slight foreign accent

"There's not even a similar modus operandi involved, or anything like it! One pushed a young broker's clerk off a terrace. The other dropped cyanide into the drink of a seedy ne'er-do-well in a mangy hotel. As far as we know, the two men not only did not know the women who brought about their deaths but had never heard of each other. No, Wanger, I think it's two entirely different cases——"

"Linked by the same murderess," Wanger insisted, unconvinced. "With these two diametrically opposite descriptions staring me in the face, I'll grant you it's like flying in the face of Providence to dispute. Just the same, all those physical differences don't mean much. Just break them down a minute, and look how easy it is to get the smallest common denominator.

"Blond and redhead: any little chorus girl will tell you how transitory that distinction can be.

"Five feet five and five seven; if one wore a pair of extra-high heels and one wore flat heels, that could still be the same girl.

"Fresh and sallow complexions: a dusting of powder takes care of that. "The difference in eye coloring can be an optical illusion created by the application of eye shadow.

"The seeming difference in age is another variable, likewise dependent on externals such as costume and manner.

"And what else is left? An accent? *I* can talk with an accent myself, if I feel like it.

"A point to remember is that no single person who saw one of these women saw the other. We have a complete set of witnesses on each of them separately. We have no single witness on the two of them at one time. There's no chance of getting a comparison. You say there's no similarity in modus operandi, but there is in every way. It's just the method of commission that was different; you're letting that mislead you. Notice these 'two' unknown women involved. Both have a brilliant, almost uncanny faculty for disappearing immediately afterward. It amounts almost to genius. Both stalk their victims ahead of time, evidently trying to get a line on their background and habits. One appeared at Bliss's flat while he was out, the other cased Mitchell's room—also while he was out. If that isn't modus operandi, what is? I tell you it's the same woman in both cases."

"What's her motive then?" his superior argued. "Not robbery. Mitchell was a month and a half behind in his room rent. She bought out an entire loge at $3.30 a seat and threw two of the seats away just to be sure of getting to meet him under favorable circumstances. Revenge would be perfect, but—he didn't know her and she didn't know him. We not only can't fit a motive to it, but we can't even apply the explanation that usually goes with lack of motive. She's not a homicidal maniac, either. She had a beautiful opportunity to kilt the Hodges girl—and the Hodges girl is the juicy, beefy, lamebrain type that's almost irresistible to a congenital murderer. Instead she passed it up, warned the girl off for the girl's own sake."

"The motive lies back in the past, way back in the past," Wanger insisted obduratcly.

"You sifted through Bliss's past—broke it down almost day by day—and couldn't find one anywhere."

"I must have missed it then. I'm to blame, not it. It was there, I didn't see it."

"We're up against something here. D'you realize that even if these two men were still alive they themselves couldn't throw any light on who she is, what she did it for—because they didn't know her themselves, seem never to have seen her before?"

"That's a thought to cheer one up," said Wanger glumly. "I can't promise you to solve this, even though you've turned it over to me. All I can promise is not to quit trying until I do."

Wanger's record on Mitchell (five months later):

Evidence: 1 envelope, typed on sample machine on display at typewriter salesroom, without knowledge of personnel.

1 arak bottle, purchased Globe Liquor Store.

1 ticket stub, Loge A-1, Elgin Theater.

Case Unsolved.

PART THREE

MORAN

Like the beat beat beat of the tom tom
When the jungle shadows fall,
Like the tick tick tock of the stately clock
As it stands against the wall—

—COLE PORTER

I

The Woman

IT WAS HIS experience that grownups always asked such dumb questions. Questions about things that were so self-evident that you yourself had long ago learned to take them for granted. But they always had to know the answer. Especially when you wanted to do something else. Something really worthwhile, like bouncing an oversize brightly colored ball along the sidewalk. Like this lady that was holding him up right now. Bending down and being so kind and all that, and keeping him from having any fun.

"My, what a big ball that is for such a little fellow."

Well, anyone could see it was a big ball. Why did she have to tell him that? Why didn't she go home where she lived?

"How old are you?"

What did she have to know how old he was for? "Five anna haff goin' on six."

"Just think. Whose little boy are you?"

What did she have to know whose little boy he was for? He wasn't hers, she ought to know that by looking at him. "My mother's and father's," he mumbled patronizingly. How could anyone be anyone else's?

"And what's your father's name, dear?" Didn't she know anything at all? She probably meant that vague, formal, never used name that his father seemed to have for an extra appendage; not the logical "daddy." "Mista Moran," he parroted.

She said something about a door. "How adorable." Then she said, "Have you any brothers and sisters?"

"Nope."

"Ah, what a shame! Don't you miss them?"

How could you miss them when you never had them? However, he could vaguely sense some sort of personal reflection involved in not having any, so he immediately tried to make good the lack with substitutes. "I got a grandma, though."

"Isn't that lovely? Does she live right with you?"

One's grandma never did, didn't she know that? "She lives in Garrison." Another substitute came to mind with that mental image, so he threw her into the gap, too. "So does my Aunt Ada, too." Wasn't she ever going to let him go ahead bouncing his ball?

"Oh, all the way up there!" she marveled. "Were you ever up there to meet her?"

"Shoe I was, when I was little. But Dr. Bixby said I made too much noise, so mommy hadda bring me back home again."

"Is Dr. Bixby your grandma's doctor, dear?"

"Shoe, he comes there lots."

"Tell me, dear, have you started school yet?"

What an insulting question! How old did she think he was anyway—*two?* "Shoe. I go to kindergarten every day," he said self-importantly.

"And what do you *do* there, dear?"

"We draw ducks and rabbits and cows. Miss Baker gave me a gol' star for drawin' a cow." Wasn't she ever going to go away and leave him be? This felt like it had kept up for hours. He could have bounced his ball all the way up to the corner and back, the time she'd made him waste.

He tried to go around one side of her, and she finally took the hint. "Well, dear, run along and play, I won't keep you any longer." She patted him twice on the bullet-shaped back of his head and moved off down the sidewalk, throwing him a fetching smile backward over her shoulder.

His mother's voice suddenly sounded through the screen of the open ground-floor window. She must have been sitting there the whole time. You could see out through the screen, but you couldn't see in through it; he'd found that out long ago. "What was the nice lady saying to you, Cookie?" she asked benevolently. A grown-up would have detected a note of instinctive pride that her offspring was so remarkable in every way he even attracted the attention of passing strangers.

"She wanned to know how ol' I was," he answered absently. He turned his attention to more important business. "Mommy, watch. Look how high I can throw this!"

"Yes, dear, but not too high, it might roll into the gutter."

A moment later he'd already forgotten the incident. Two moments later his mother had.

II

Moran

MORAN'S WIFE HAD called up the office while he was out to lunch; there was a message from her waiting there for him when he got back.

This didn't startle him; it was a fairly frequent occurrence, on an average of every third day. Something she'd found out she needed from downtown and wanted him to stop off and get for her on his way home, most likely, he thought at first. Then on second thought he saw it couldn't quite be that, either, or, having failed to reach him, she would have simply left the message with the switchboard girl. Unless, of course, it was something that needed more detailed instructions than could be conveniently conveyed at secondhand.

He made use of his brief after-lunch digestive torpor to phone. "Here's your wife, Mr. Moran."

"Frank—" Margaret's voice sounded emotionally charged, so he knew right away, before she'd got any further than his name, that this was more than just a purchase errand.

"H'lo, dear, what's up?"

"Oh, Fuh-rank, I'm awfully glad you got back! I'm worried

sick, I don't know what to do. I just got a telegram from Ada half an hour ago——"

Ada was her unmarried sister, upstate. "A telegram?" he said. "Why a telegram?"

"Well, that's just it. Here, I'll read it to you." It took her a moment or two; she must have had to fumble for it in her apron pocket and unfold it with one hand "It says, 'Mother down with bad spell, don't want to frighten you but suggest you come at once, Dr. Bixby agrees. Don't delay. Ada.'"

"I suppose it's her heart again," he said somewhat less than compassionately. Why'd she have to bother him in the middle of the business day with something like this?

She had begun to whimper in a low-keyed restrained way that was not quite outright weeping—a sort of frightened watering of her conversation. "Frank, what'll I do? D'you think I ought to call them up long-distance?"

"If she wants you to go up there, you better go up there," he answered shortly.

She'd evidently wanted to hear this advice; it chimed in with her own inclinations. "I guess I'd better," she agreed tearfully. "You know Ada, she's anything but an alarmist, she's always been inclined to minimize these things before now. The last time mother had one of her spells she didn't even let me know about it until it was all over, to keep from worrying me."

"Don't get so unnerved about it. Your mother's had these spells before and gotten over them," he tried to point out.

But her distress had already taken a different tack. "But what'll I do about you and Cookie?"

He took umbrage at being lumped together with his five-year-old son in helplessness. "I can look after him," he said sharply. "I'm no cripple. Do you want me to find out what buses there are for you?"

"I've already done that myself, and there's one at five. If I take a later one I'll have to sit up all night, and you know how miserable that is."

"You better take the early one," he agreed.

The pace of her conversation quickened, became a flurry. "I'm all packed—just an overnight bag. Now, Frank, will you meet me at the terminal?"

"Okay, okay." He was starting to get a little impatient with this endless rigmarole. Women didn't know how to make a telephone call short and to the point. His secretary was standing in the doorway, waiting to consult him about something.

"And, Frank, be sure you're there on time. Remember, you'll have to take Cookie home with you. I'll have him with me; I'm picking him up at the kindergarten on my way downtown."

As punctual as he made it a point to be, Margaret was already there ahead of him when he got down to the terminal, with the little dab of foreshortened humanity that was Cookie by her side. The latter began to jump up and down, giving vertical emphasis to the important information he had to impart. "Daddy, mommy's going away! Mommy's going away!"

He was unnoticed by both of them, this being one of the rare times he didn't succeed in monopolizing the opening moments of one of their conversations. "What've you been doing, crying?" Moran accused her. "Sure you have, I can tell by your eyes. There's no sense acting that way about it."

A torrent of maternal advice began pouring from her. "Now, Frank, you'll find the food for his supper all ready on the kitchen table, all you'll have to do is heat it. And, Frank, don't feed him too late, it isn't good for him. Oh, and another thing, you'd better let him do without his bath tonight. You don't know enough about giving it to him, and I'm afraid something might happen to him in the tub."

"One night without it won't kill him," Moran grunted contemptuously. "And, Frank, do you think you'll know how to undress him?"

"Sure. Just unbutton, and there you are. What's the difference between his things and my own? Just smaller, that's all."

But the torrent spilled forth unabated. "And, Frank, if you should want to go out yourself later on, I wouldn't leave him alone in the house if I were you. Maybe you can get one of the neighbors to come in and give him an eye——"

A voice was megaphoning sepulchrally somewhere in the vaulted depths below the waiting room. "Hobbs Landing, Allenville, Greendale——"

"That's yours, y'better get on."

They moved slowly down the ramp to departure level. The torrent was at last slackening; it came only in desultory little spurts now, afterthoughts concerned with his own personal well-being. "Now, Frank, you know where I keep your clean shirts and things——"

"Ba-awd," the bus starter was keening.

She wound her arms about his neck with unexpected tightness, as though she were still not one hundred percent maternal. "Goodbye, Frank, I'll be back the minute I can."

"Phone me when you get up there so I'll know you arrived okay."

"I do hope she'll be all right."

"Sure she will, she'll be up and around again before the week is out——"

She crouched down by Cookie, adjusted his cap, his jacket collar, the hem of one of his little knee pants, kissed him on the three sides of the head. "Now, Cookie, you be a good boy, listen to whatever daddy tells you." The last thing she said, from inside the bus steps, was, "Frank, he's forming a habit of telling little fibs lately, I've been trying to break him of it; don't encourage him——"

She finally had to turn away because others were trying to get in after her and she was blocking the entrance. The bus driver turned his head and followed her morosely with his eyes down the aisle toward her seat. He muttered, "For Pete's sake, I only run a couple of hours upstate, not all the way to the Mexican border."

Moran and offspring shifted over on the platform opposite her seat. She couldn't get the window up, or she would probably have gone on indefinitely in the same vein as before. She had to content herself with blowing kisses and making instructive signs to the two of them through the pane. Moran couldn't tell what most of them meant but pretended he understood by nodding docilely in order to make her feel better about it.

The bus started to wheel out along the concrete with a gritty, hissing sound. Moran bent down to the diminutive self beside him, raised one of its toothpick arms. "Wave goodbye to your mother," he instructed. He worked the little appendage awkwardly back and forth, like something on a toy pump.

He was thinking of Margaret for the tenth time, with a newborn respect, almost with awe, for being able to whip any kind of results out of chaos like this—and not just once, but day after day—when the doorbell rang.

He groaned aloud. "I haven't got enough on my hands, I gotta have company yet, to hang around and laugh at me!"

He had his coat and tie off, shirt sleeves rolled up out of harm's way, and one of Margaret's aprons tucked into his belt. He'd managed to get Cookie's food warmed up—after all, the way Margaret had left it waiting, all you did was strike a match and put it on the gas stove—and he'd managed to bring Cookie and the food together at the table, after a lot of running around. But accomplishment ended there. What did you do to keep a kid from walloping it backhand with the flat of his spoon, making mud pies with it so to speak, so that it flew up all over? With Margaret around, Cookie just seemed to eat. With him, he laid down barrages on it, and flecks of it were even hitting the wall opposite.

Moran kept shifting around behind him from one side to the other, trying to nab the niblick shots that were doing all the damage. Persuasion was worse than useless; Cookie had him out on a limb and knew it.

The door bell peeped a second time. Moran meanwhile being so busy he had already forgotten about the first ring. He raked despairing fingers through his hair, looked from Cookie out toward the door and from the door back to Cookie. Finally, as though deciding nothing could be any worse than this, he started out to answer it, wiping off a dab of spinach from just above one eyebrow.

It was a woman, and he didn't know her. She was a lady, anyway; she carefully refrained from seeming to see the apron with blue forget-me-nots in one corner, acted as though he looked perfectly normal.

She was young and rather pretty but was dressed in a way that seemed deliberately to seek to ignore the latter attribute; in a neat but plain blue serge jacket and skirt. Her hair was red-dish gold and kept in severe confinement by pins or some other means. Her face was innocent of anything but soap and water. She had a little rosette of freckles on each cheek, high up on it; none anywhere else. She had an almost boyish air of friendliness and naturalness.

"Is this Cookie Moran's house?" she asked with a friendly little smile.

"Yes—but my wife's away right now . . ." Moran answered helplessly, wondering what she wanted.

"I know, Mr. Moran." There was something understanding, almost commiserating, about the way she said it. There was also a betraying little twitch at the corner of her mouth, quickly re-strained, "She said something about that when she came by for Cookie. That's why I'm here. I'm Cookie's kindergarten teacher, Miss Baker."

"Oh, yes!" he said quickly, recognizing the name. "I've heard my wife speak of you a lot." They shook hands; she had the firm, cordial sort of a grip you would have expected her to have.

"Mrs. Moran didn't actually ask me to come over, but I could tell by the way she spoke she was worried about how you two would make out, so I took it upon myself to do it anyway. I know she's had to leave on fairly short notice, so if there's any-thing I can do——"

He didn't make any bones about showing his relief and grati-tude. "Say, that's swell of you!" he said fervently. "Are you a life-saver, Miss Baker! Come in——"

He became belatedly aware of the forget-me-notted apron, snatched it off and hid it behind him bunched in one hand.

"How do you get them to eat, anyway?" he asked confidentially, closing the door and following her down the hall. "I'm afraid to ram it in his mouth, he might choke——"

"I know just how it is, Mr. Moran, I know just how it is," she said consolingly. She took one all-comprehensive look around her when she got to the dining-room doorway and gave a deep-throated little chuckle. "I can see I got here just in the nick of time." He'd thought it was in pretty good shape until now, compared to the kitchen. That was where the hurricane had really struck.

"How's the young man?" she asked.

"Cookie, look who's here," Moran said, still overjoyed at this unexpected succor that was like manna from heaven. "Miss Baker, your kindergarten teacher. Aren't you going to say hello to her?"

Cookie studied her a long moment with the grave unblinking eyes of childhood. "Is not!" he finally said dispassionately.

"Why, Cookie!" Miss Baker rebuked gently. She crouched down by the high chair, bringing her head to the level of his. She put a finger to his chin and guided it. "Turn around and look at me good." She found time to flash a tolerant smile to Moran over his head. "Don't you know Miss Baker anymore?"

Moran was embarrassed for the child, as though it made him out the parent of a mentally retarded offspring. "Cookie, what's the matter with you, don't you know your own kindergarten teacher?"

"Is not," said Cookie without taking his eyes off her.

Miss Baker looked at the father, completely at a loss. "What do you suppose it is?" she asked solicitously. "He's never been that way with me before."

"I dunno, unless—unless—" A remark his wife had made

came back to him. "Margaret warned me just now before she left that he's starting to tell little fibs; maybe this is one of them now." He put an edge of authority into his voice for his auditor's benefit. "Now, see here, young man——"

She made a charming little secretive gesture with her eyelids, a sort of deprecating flicker. "Let me handle him," she breathed. "I'm used to them." You could see she was a person who had infinite patience with children, would never lose her temper under any circumstances. She thrust her face toward him cajolingly. "What's the matter, Cookie, don't you know me anymore? I know you."

Cookie wasn't saying.

"Wait, I think I have something here." She opened her large handbag, brought out a folded sheet of paper. Spread, it revealed an outline drawing, printed, filled in with crayon coloring by hand. The crayon filling did not match the guidelines very accurately, but the will was there.

Cookie eyed it without any visible signs of pride of accomplishment. "Don't you remember doing this for me this morning—and, I told you how good it was? Don't you remember you got a gold star for doing this?"

That, at least, had a familiar ring to Moran's own ears, if not his offspring's. Many a night on coming home he'd gotten the vertically ejaculated tidings, "I got a gol' star today!"

"Are you Miss Baker?" Cookie conceded warily.

"Ho!" She worried the lobe of his ear. "Of course I am, bless you! *You* know that,"

"Then why don't you look like she does?"

She smiled amusedly at Moran. "I suppose he means the glasses. He's used to my wearing horn-rimmed glasses when teaching class; I came out without them tonight. There's a fine point of child psychology involved, too. He's used to seeing me in the kindergarten and not in his home. I don't belong here. So—" she spread her hands "—I'm not the same person."

Moran was secretly admiring her scientific attitude toward the child and the thorough knowledge it was obviously grounded on, so different from Margaret's irrational, emotional approach.

She stood up, evidently not a believer in pressing a contested point too far with a reluctant child at any one given time; rather winning it over to her viewpoint by degrees, a little at a time. He'd heard Margaret say that was the way they handled the youngsters at the kindergarten.

"He'll forget all about this refusal to recognize me himself in five minutes—watch, you'll see," she promised brightly in an undertone.

"You've got to know just how to go about it with kids, don't you?" he said, impressed.

"They're distinct little entities in their own right, you know, not just half-formed grown-ups. That's a mistaken old-fashioned notion that we've discarded." She removed her hat and jacket, started toward the ravaged kitchen. "Now, let me see what I can do here to help. How about you yourself, Mr. Moran?"

"Oh, never mind about me," he said with insincere self-denial. "I can go out to a cafeteria later——"

"Nonsense, there's no need for that at all, I'll have something ready before you know it. Now, you just read your evening paper—I can see by the way it's still folded over you haven't had a chance to go near it yet—and just forget everything, as though your wife were here looking after things."

She was, thought Moran with a grateful sigh, one of the nicest, most competent, most considerate young women to have around that he'd ever yet had the pleasure of encountering. He strolled out into the living room, rolled down his shirt sleeves and eased back behind his evening box score.

It seemed a longer ride than it had the summer before, when she and Frank had last made the trip up, although Garrison hadn't moved any at one end, or the city at the other. But that was because she was making it alone, for one thing, she supposed, and under unfavorable auspices, for another.

Frank had got her a seat by the window, and no one came to claim the one beside her, so she was spared the added discomfort of having to keep up a desultory conversation with some well-meaning seatmate; the penalty for refusal being, as she knew only too well, the even greater discomfort of sitting in strained, hostile awareness of each other after the preliminary snub.

The countryside spilled past with the rippling motion of overturned earth, as though the bus were plowing a steady furrow through it but carrying its trees, houses, fences along with it intact. She saw it only with the physical surface of her eye, it wasn't transmitted through the iris. Every twelve minutes, regularly, she remembered something she'd forgotten to tell Frank about Cookie or the house or the milkman or the laundryman. But then—and she realized this herself—even if she had remembered in the first place and told him, he probably would have forgotten it himself by now. That docile nodding outside the bus window hadn't fooled her; it had been too facile.

Between the twelve-minute intervals she did a lot of worrying about her mother. The way one does, anyone does.

But she realized she was only making herself feel worse, borrowing trouble ahead of time, writing an obituary, so to speak, before there was any need to. As Frank said, it would be all right. It had to be. And if—God forbid—it turned out not to be in the end, then rushing to meet it halfway was no help, either.

She tried to shorten the trip, take her mind off its purpose, by thinking of other things. It was not easy to do. She had not the pictorial eye; inanimate scenery had never meant much to her. And since, on the other hand, she had never taken a passionate interest in the study of human nature in the abstract, what else was there left on a vehicle of this sort? She wondered if it would have helped if she'd bought a book or magazine at the terminal and brought it with her. Probably not; it would have remained opened on her lap at one certain page the whole way. She'd never been any great shakes as a reader.

In desperation that was almost pathetic she started to tally up her household expenses for the past week, and then for the past two weeks. The figures blurred in her mind, became fantastically senseless. She could not forget the hard little knot of worry that lay heavy within her.

It had grown dark now, and the view became restricted to the midget, tubular world she was confined in. The other people around her in the bus were—the other people usually around in a bus. No sublimation to be found there. Just the backs of heads.

She sighed and wished she were an Indian or whatever those people were who could leave their bodies and get there ahead of where they were going. Or something like that, anyway; she wasn't sure of the mechanics of it.

Around eight they stopped at Greendale for ten minutes, and she had a cup of coffee at the counter in the bus station. As far as Cookie was concerned, at home, the worst was already over by this time, she realized. Either he had a bad case of stomachache by now or else Frank had fed him the way he should be fed and there was nothing further to worry about.

It seemed needless to phone ahead to Garrison from here; she was already two-thirds of the way there. And then there was always the thought that if she should get worse news than she'd already had in the telegram, it would make the rest of the trip an unendurable torment. It was better to wait until she got there herself to find out.

They arrived strictly on schedule, ten-thirty on the dot. She was the first one down, elbowing her way through the other passengers.

She wasn't disappointed that there was no one waiting to meet her, because she realized Ada must have her hands full at the house; it couldn't be expected at such a time.

Garrison's brief, foreshortened nightlife was in mid-career immediately outside the bus station. Which meant the movie-theater entrance was still lighted on one side of the way and the drugstore on the other.

She passed a group of chattering young girls in their late teens and early twenties holding down a section of the board sidewalk just outside the drugstore entrance. One of them turned her head to look after her as she went by, and she heard her say, "Isn't that Margaret Peabody—now?"

She hurried along the plank walk, head lowered, into the surrounding darkness. Luckily they didn't yoo-hoo after her to try to make sure. She didn't want to stop and talk to near strangers. They might have news. She didn't want to hear it from them first. She wanted to go straight home and get it there, good or bad. But that "now," it hung trembling over her, roaring in her mind. What did it mean, that it was already . . . ?

She hurried up the dark tunnellike length of Burgoyne

Street, smothered under trees, turned left, continued on for two house lengths (which here meant two city blocks, very nearly), turned in at the well-remembered flagstone walk with its tricky unevenness of edges. Each one went up a fraction of an inch higher than the one adjoining. Many a fall in childhood's awkward days——

She caught her breath with a quick little suction as the house swiveled around full face to her. Oh, yes, oh, yes, there were too many lights lit, far too many. Then she curbed her mounting panic, forced it down. Well, even—even if mother was laid up in bed at all with the slightest of attacks, Ada would have more than the usual number of lights lit, wouldn't she? She'd have to, to be able to look after her.

But then as she stepped up on the little white-painted porch platform, dread assailed her again. There were too many shadows flitting back and forth behind the lowered linen shades, you could hear the hum of too many voices coming from inside, as at a time of crisis, when neighbors are called in. There was something wrong in there, there was some sort of commotion going on.

She reached out and poked the bell button with an icicle for a finger. Instantly the commotion became aggravated. A voice screamed, "I'll go!" Another shrieked, "No, let me!" She could hear them clearly out where she was. Had one of them been Ada's, high-pitched and unrecognizable with uncontrollable grief? It seemed to her it had. She must be hysterical, all of them must be.

Before her heart had time to turn over and drop down through her like a rock, there was a quick shuffle of frenzied footsteps, as though someone was trying to hold someone else back. The door billowed open and a great gush of yellow interi-

or light fanned out all over her. There were two unrecognizable figures silhouetted in it, grotesques with strange shapes on their heads.

"I got to it first!" the smaller one proclaimed jubilantly.

"I was opening doors before you were born——" The music and the welter of hilarious voices streamed out around them into the quiet country night.

Her heart didn't drop, her overnight bag did instead—with a slap to the porch floor. "Mother," she gasped soundlessly.

The other figure in the paper party cap was Ada. "Margaret, you darling! How did you remember it was my birthday? Oh, what a dandy surprise, I couldn't have asked for anything——"

They were talking at cross-purposes, the three of them. "Oh, but Ada——" Margaret Moran was remonstrating in a shaky, smothered voice, still unmanageable from the unexpected shock. "How could you do it *that* way! If you knew what I went through on the way up here! No, mother's health is one thing I don't think you have any right to joke about. Frank won't like it a bit when he hears it!"

A puzzled silence had fallen over the two standing in the doorway. They turned to look after her. She was inside in the crepe-paper-lighted hallway now. The vivacious old lady asked Ada with a birdlike, quizzical cock of her head, "What does she mean?"

Ada asked at the same time, "What on earth is she talking about?"

"I got a telegram from you at one this afternoon. You told me mother'd had another of her attacks, and to come at once. You even mentioned Dr. Bixby's name in it——" Margaret Moran had begun to cry a little with indignation, a natural reaction from the long strain she had been under.

The mother said, "Dr. Bixby's in there now; I was just danc-ing a cakewalk with him, wasn't I, Ada?"

Her sister's face had gone white under the flush of the party excitement. She took a step backward. "I never in the world sent you any telegram!" she gasped.

Moran surreptitiously stuck a thumb under the waistband of his trousers to gain a little additional slack. "Margaret couldn't have done any better herself," he said wholeheartedly, "and when I say that, I'm giving you all the praise I know how.

"It'll make her your friend for life when I tell her how you walked in here and saved the day. You must come over and have dinner with the two of us—I mean without working for it—when she gets back."

She eyed the empty plates with a cook's instinctive approval, flattered to see that her efforts have not been slighted. "Thank you," she said, "I'd love to. I don't get as much home cooking as I might myself. I've had a room at the Women's Club since I've had this school job, and there are no facilities. Before then, of course, at home, we all took turns in the kitchen."

She rose slowly, stacked the dishes together. "Now you just sit there and take it easy, Mr. Moran, or inside in the next room or wherever you please. I'll get through these in no time."

"You could leave them in there," he remonstrated. "Marga-ret's cleaning lady comes tomorrow, and she'll do them."

"Oh, well," she shrugged deprecatingly, "it's not much trou-ble, and one thing I can't bear to see left lying around is dirty dishes, in my own or anybody else's kitchen. I'll be all finished before you know it."

She was going to make some lucky stiff a mighty fine lit-tle wife one of these days, Moran thought, watching her bustle back and forth; the wonder of it was she hadn't already. What was the matter with the young fellows around these parts, didn't they have eyes in their heads?

He went into the living room, turned on the double-globed reading lamp and sat down with his paper, to give it a second and more exhaustive going-over. It was just as good as though Margaret were home, really; you could hardly tell the difference. Except maybe that she didn't say, "Don't" to Cookie quite so often. Maybe too much of that wasn't good for a kid. She was a teacher, she ought to know.

She came out to the dining-room door one time and spoke to him, drying a large dish between her hands with a cloth. "Nearly through now," she announced cheerfully. "How're you two getting along in here?"

"Fine," said Moran, looking back across his shoulder at her from the semireclining slope the chair gave him, "I'm waiting to hear from my wife; she promised to call as soon as she gets up there and let me know how things are."

"That won't be for some time yet, will it?"

He glanced at the clock across the room. "Not much before ten-thirty or eleven, I guess."

She said, "I'm going to squeeze out some orange juice for the two of you, for the morning, as soon as I finish putting the last of these away. I'll leave it in a glass inside the Frigidaire."

"Aw, you don't have to bother doing that——"

"Doesn't take a minute; Cookie really should have it daily, you know. It's the best thing for them." She returned to the kitchen again.

Moran shook his head to himself. What a paragon.

Cookie was in there with him just then, playing around. Then a minute or so later he got up and went to the hall door, stood there looking out, talking to her. She'd evidently wandered out there herself, from the kitchen door at the other end of it, while she finished drying the last of the utensils. Margaret had that habit, too, of perambulating around when she was in the last stages of drying.

Cookie was standing perfectly still, watching her. He heard him say, "What're you doing that for?"

"To dry it off, dear," she answered with cheery forthrightness.

Moran heard it only subconsciously, so to speak, with the fraction of those faculties not absorbed in his paper.

She came in a moment later, painstakingly wiping the blade of a small sharp-edge fruit knife that she'd evidently just used to cut and prepare the oranges.

Cookie's eyes followed the deft motions of her hands with that hypnotic concentration children can bring to bear on the most trivial actions at times. Once he turned his head and glanced back into the hallway, somewhere beyond the radius of the door, where she had been just now, with equally rapt absorption. Then back to her again.

"There, all through," she said to him playfully, flicking the end of the dishcloth toward him. "Now I'll play with you for five or ten minutes, and then we'll see about putting you to bed."

Moran looked up at this point, out of sheer sense of duty. "Sure there's nothing I can do to help?" he asked, hoping against hope the answer would be no.

It was. "You go right back to your paper," she said with friendly authoritativeness. "This young man and I are going to have a little game of hide-and-seek."

She was certainly a godsend. Why, when it came to getting your paper read without distraction, she was even better to have around than Margaret. Margaret seemed to think you could read your paper and carry on a conversation with her at one and the same time. So either you had to be a surly bear or you had to read each paragraph twice, and slowly, once as a gentle hint and once for the meaning.

Not that he was being disloyal about it; rather have Margaret, bless her, conversational interruptions or not.

Ada tried to silence the buzzing party guests. "Shh! Be quiet just a minute, everybody. Margaret's out in the hall, trying to call her husband in the city and tell him about it." She took the added precaution of drawing the two sliding parlor doors together.

"From here?" one of the younger girls piped up incredulously. "For heaven's sake, that costs money!"

"I know, but she's all upset about it, and I don't blame her. Who could have done such a thing? Why, that's a horrible trick to play on anyone!"

One of the matrons said with unshakable local pride, "I know nobody up here in our community would be capable of it. We all think too much of Delia Peabody and her girls." Then immediately spoiled it by adding, "Not even Cora Hopkins. . . ."

"And they signed my *name* to it!" Ada protested dramatically. "It must be somebody that knows the family."

"And mine, too, isn't that what she said?" Dr. Bixby added. "Where'd they hear about me?"

Half-frightened little glances were exchanged here and there about the room, as though somebody had just told a chilling ghost story. One of the girls, perched on the windowsill, looked behind her into the dark, then stood up and furtively moved deeper into the room. "It's like a poison-pen tellygram," somebody breathed in a husky stage whisper.

Ada had reopened the sliding doors a foot, overcome by her own curiosity. "Did you get him yet?" she asked through them. "What does he say?"

Margaret Moran appeared in the opening, widened it and then stayed in it undecidedly. "She said our house doesn't answer. He *could* be out, but— look at the time. And if he is, what's he done with Cookie? He wouldn't have him out with him at this hour. And the last thing he said was he wouldn't budge out of the house. There ought to be someone there with Cookie to watch him. . . ."

She looked helplessly from Ada to her mother to the doctor, who were the three nearest to her. "I don't like it. Don't you think I ought to start back——"

A chorus of concerned protest went up. "Now?"

"Why, you just stepped off one bus, you'll be dead!"

"Ah, Margaret, why don't you wait over until the morning at least?"

"It isn't that—it's that telegram. I don't know, it gives me a creepy feeling, I can't shake it off. A thing like that isn't funny, it's—it's malicious; there's something almost dangerous about it. Anyone that would do that— well, there's no telling *what*——"

"Why don't you try just once more," the old family doctor suggested soothingly. "Maybe he's gotten back in the meantime. Then, if he hasn't and you still feel like going, I'll drive you over to the bus station; my car's right outside now."

This time they didn't bother closing the doors at all; they didn't have to be told to be quiet. With one accord they all shifted out into the hall after her and fanned out in a wide half circle, ringing her and the telephone around, listening in breathless sympathetic silence. It was as though she were holding a public audition for her innermost wifely distress.

Her voice shook a little. "Operator, get me the city again. That same number—Seville 7-6262."

From time to time he could hear a splatter of quick running footsteps somewhere nearby, and a burst of crowing laughter from Cookie, and an "I see you!" from her. Mostly up and down the hall out there.

Hide-and-seek, he supposed tolerantly. They said there were two things that never changed, death and taxes; they should have added a third— children's games. Even this she seemed to be able to go about in a soothing, fairly subdued way, without letting the kid be too boisterous about it. Must be the professional touch, that. He wondered how much kindergarten teachers earned. She was certainly good.

One time there was a stealthy, stalking cessation of sound a little more long-drawn-out than the others, and he looked up to find her hiding herself just within the room doorway. She was standing with her back to him, peeping out around it into the hall. "Ready?" she called genially. Cookie's answer came back with unexpected faintness. "Not yet—wait."

She seemed to enjoy it as much as the kid. That was the right way to play with them, he supposed—put your whole heart and soul into it. Children were quick to spot lack of enthusiasm. You could tell Cookie was already crazy about her. He was evidently seeing her in a different light than he had in the school, where she had to maintain a certain amount of discipline.

She turned her head, found him watching her approving-ly. "He's gone into that little storage space built in beneath the staircase," she confided with a twinkle. And then, more seriously, "Is it safe for him to go in there?"

"Safe?" repeated Moran blankly. "Sure—there's nothing in there, couple of old raincoats."

"Ready," a faint voice called.

She turned her head. "Here I come," she warned, and vanished from the doorway as unnoticeably as she had first appeared in it.

He could hear her pretendedly questing here and there for a preliminary moment or two, to keep up the relish of the game longer. Then a straining at woodwork and a muffled burst of gleeful acknowledgment.

Suddenly his name sounded with unexpected tautness. "Mr. Moran!" He jumped up and started out to them. It had been that kind of a tone: *hurry*. She'd repeated it twice before he could even reach them, short as the distance was.

She was pulling at the old-fashioned iron handgrip riveted to the door. Her face was whitening down around the chin and mouth. "I can't get it open—see, that's what I meant a minute ago!"

"Now, don't get frightened," he calmed her. "There's nothing to it." He grasped the iron handgrip, simply pulled it up a half inch parallel to the door, the latch tongue freed itself, and he drew out the heavy oaken panel. It was set into the back of the staircase structure, half the height of the average door and a little broader. It did not quite meet the floor, either; there was a half-foot sill under it.

Cookie clambered out hilariously.

"See what it was? You were trying to pull it out toward you.

It works on a spring latch and you have to free that first by hitching the iron bracket up; then you pull it out."

"I see that now. Stupid of me," she said half-shamefacedly. She gestured vaguely above her heart, fanned a hand before her face. "I didn't let on to you, but what a fright it gave me! Phew! I was afraid it had jammed and he'd smother in there before we could——"

"Oh, I'm sorry . . . darn shame . . ." he said contritely, as if it had been his fault for having such a door in his house at all.

She seemed to want to continue to discuss possibilities, as though there was a hidden morbid streak in her. "I suppose if worse had come to worst, you could have broken it down, though, at a moment's notice,"

"I could have taken something to it, yes," he agreed.

She seemed surprised. He saw her eye glance appraisingly over his husky upper torso. "Couldn't you have broken it down with your bare hands or by crashing your shoulder against it?"

He fingered the edge of the door, guided it outward so she could scan it. "Oh, no. This is solid oak. Two inches thick. Look at that. Well-built house, you know. And it's in a bad place; there isn't room enough on either side to run against it, to get up impetus. The turn of the wall here only gives you a couple yards of space. And on the inside it slants down with the incline of the stairs; you can't even stand up full-length. The closet's triangular, wedge shaped, see? Swing your arm too far back over your shoulder, on either side of the door, and it would jam against the sloping top. Or against the wall indentation out here."

Suddenly, to his surprise, she had lowered her head, gone through the low doorway into the darkness inside. He could hear her sounding the thick sides of it with her palms. She came out again in a moment. "Isn't it well built!" she marveled. "But it's stuffy in there, even with the door open. How long do you suppose a person could last if they did actually happen to get themselves locked into such a place?"

His masculine omniscience was caught unprepared for once. He'd evidently never given the matter any thought before. "Oh, I don't know . . ." he said vaguely. "Hour and a half, two hours at the most." He looked up and down the thing with abstract interest. "It is pretty air-tight, at that," he conceded.

She winced repugnantly at this thought she had herself conjured up, wholesomely changed the subject. Everyone, after all, has odd moments of morbid conjecture. She leaned down, grasped Cookie from below the armpits and started to march his legs stiffly out before him like a mechanical soldier. "Well, mister." Then she deferred to Moran: "Do you think he should go to bed now?"

Cookie started some more vertical emphasis. He was having too good a time to give it up without a battle. "One more! One more!"

"All right, just one more and then that's all," she conceded indulgently. Moran went back to his chair in the living room. He'd finished his paper.

Exhaustively; even down to the quotations of stocks he didn't own but would have liked to. Even down to letters from readers on topics that didn't interest him. He took out a cigar the man he'd lunched with had given him today, appraised it, accepted it for smoking, stripped it and lit it up. He blew a lariat of sky blue around his head with ineffable comfort. He sat there with it for a moment in a complete vacuum of contentment.

It was a seldom enjoyed luxury, and he almost didn't know what to do with it. His head started to nod. He caught it the first time, took time off to put his cigar on the tray beside him so he wouldn't drop it and burn a hole in Margaret's carpet.

Cookie came tiptoeing in with exaggerated mincing of footfalls that was almost a hobbling creep, probably impressed upon him from outside, carrying Moran's soft-toed carpet slippers, one in each hand. Soft toed and soft soled. "Miss Baker says to put these on, you feel better," he whispered sibilantly.

"Say, that's fine," Moran beamed. He bent down and effected the change. "Tell her she's spoiling me."

Cookie tiptoed out with the discarded shoes—heavy soled, thick toed—with as much precaution as when he'd come in, even though the object of his care was unmistakably still awake.

Moran sprawled back and, when the second and third nods came, let them ride. A girl like that oughta . . . oughta be in a jewelry-store window . . . mmmmmm. . . .

He meant well, but oh, God, it was like being on the rack to have to sit there beside him and listen to him. "Yessir, I brought all three of you girls into the world. I can remember the night you came as clear as though 'twere yesterday. And now look at you, sitting here beside me, all grown up and married and with a youngster of your own——"

And frightened, oh, how frightened, she thought dismally, eyes straining for the bus that seemed never to come.

"Doesn't seem possible. No sir, either you grew up too fast or I don't feel old enough for my age, must be one or the other."

She matched her chortle with a wan smile by the faint light of the dashboard.

"I know," he purred. He reached out and grasped her outside shoulder and juggled it hearteningly. "I know. You're all worried and upset and wish you were down there already. Now, honey, don't take on like that. It'll be all right, it's bound to be, how could it help being otherwise? Just 'cause he doesn't answer the telephone? Shucks, he's probably over at one of the neighbors' houses guzzling beer——"

"I know, Dr. Bixby, but I can't help it. It's that telegram. It gives me the most uncanny feeling, and I can't throw it off. Somebody sent that telegram——"

"Nat-chelly, nat-chelly," he chuckled benevolently, "telegrams don't just send themselves. Maybe some blame fool in his office thought he'd like to get back at him. . . ." But he let the thought die out; it wasn't very convincing.

She was staring ahead, down the state highway that skirted the opposite side of the bus station to where the doctor had his Ford parked. "It's late, isn't it? Maybe there aren't going to be any more tonight. . . ." She kept continually putting a finger to her teeth, replacing it a moment later with another one.

Dr. Bixby good-naturedly drew her hand down, held it pressed to her lap. "I broke you of that habit when you were seven; you're not going to make me do it all over again, are you?" He looked ahead through his none-too-spotless windshield. "Here she comes now. See those two lights way off down there? Yep, that must be her, all right."

Something soft brushing against his legs down by the floor roused him. He brought the point of his chin up off the second button of his shirt, looked down blurredly.

Cookie was scampering around down there on all fours like a little animal, head almost lower than his feet. "Still trying to find someplace to hide?" Moran asked fondly.

His young son looked up, sharply corrected his failure to

keep abreast of current events. "We not playing *now* anymore. Miss Baker los' her ring, I'm he'ping her to fine it."

Her voice sounded somewhere outside at that moment. "See it yet, dear?"

Moran roused himself, got up and went out. He remembered seeing it on her when she first came in.

The stair-closet door was wide open, as though she'd already been in there. She was exploring the baseboard across the way, on the opposite side of the hall, slightly bent forward, hands cupped to knees.

"I don't know how it happened to slip off without my feeling it," she said. "Oh, it's probably around somewhere. The only reason I'd feel bad about losing it is my mother gave it to me on my graduation. . . ."

"How about in here?" he said. "Have you looked in here? You stepped in here once, remember, and thumped the sides."

She glanced casually over her shoulder while she continued her search. "I looked in there already, but I didn't have any matches, so it was hard to make sure——"

"Wait a minute, I've got some right here, I'll look again for you. . . ." He stepped across the sill, struck a tarnished gold glow, crouched down with his back to the entrance.

The sound the door made was like a pistol shot echoing up and down the enclosed hallway.

III

Postmortem on Moran

Superior to Wanger:

"Well, what'dja find out over there? You seem to be becoming our expert in murders-that-don't-look-like-murders but are."

"Sure it was! Certainly it was! How can there be any doubt about it?"

"All right, don't blow all these papers off my desk. Well, Kling tells me the men he put on it don't seem to feel as sure about that as you do yourself. That's why I got his okay on your horning in. He was very nice about it——"

"What?" Wanger became almost inarticulate. "What're they trying to do, build it up that he locked himself in acci——"

His superior sliced his hand at him calmingly. "Now, wait a minute, don't get so touchy. Here's what he means by that, and I can see his point, too. It's true that Mrs. Moran got, or claims she got, an anonymous telegram with her sister's name signed to it. Unfortunately, there hasn't been any trace of it found around the house; it's disappeared, so there's no way of tracing where it was filed from. It may have been filed right here in the city, and in her perturbation she didn't notice the dateline. It's true that the kid keeps prattling about a 'lady' playing games with him. The only two facts that point definitely to an adult agency's being involved are the cut telephone wire and the note on the kid's quilt——"

Wanger forced up his underlip scornfully. "And what about the putty?"

"Meaning the kid couldn't have reached the top of the door with it, that it? No, Kling tells me they tried him out on that. Didn't interfere, just handed him the putty set, said, 'Let's see you cover up the door like the other night,' stood back and watched. When he'd gotten as high up as he could go, he dragged over the three-legged telephone stool, climbed up on that, and his hands spanned the top crack beautifully. Now if he did that, of his own accord and without being coached, the second time, why, they wanna know, couldn't he have done it the first?"

"Hoch!" Wanger cleared his throat disgustedly.

"They put him to another test. They said to him, 'Sonny, if your daddy went in there, what would you do—let him out or make him stay in?' He said, 'Make him stay in there and play a game with me.'"

"Are those guys crazy—where're their heads? I suppose the kid cut the phone wire, too. I suppose he wrote out that note in printed capitals——"

"Let me finish, will you? They're not trying to say that the kid did all those things himself. But they *are* inclined to think along the lines of it being an accident, with a clumsy frightened attempt on someone's part, afterward, to escape being involved.

"Now here's the theory of Kling's men—and remember, it

hasn't jelled, they're just playing around with it until something better shows up: Moran had some lady friend on the side. A fake telegram was sent to the wife to clear the coast. Before the woman got there, Moran, alone in the house with his kid, started playing games with him. He accidentally locked himself in the closet and the damn-fool kid puttied up the door. The woman shows up and Moran is smothered to death in there. She loses her head, deathly afraid of being dragged into it because of her reputation. She puts the kid to bed and leaves an unsigned note pinned to the quilt for the wife. Maybe the phone starts ringing while she's there, and, afraid to answer it, she loses her head even further and cuts the wire. They think she even went so completely haywire that after having already opened the closet door once and seen that Moran was dead, she made a panicky attempt to leave things looking just like she found them by closing the door on him a second time and leaving him in there, even replugging the putty so it would look like the kid's work and nobody else's. In other words, an accident followed by a clumsy attempt at concealment on the part of somebody with a guilty conscience."

"Pew!" said Wanger succinctly, pinching the end of his nose. "Well, here's the theory of your man Wanger: bull fertilizer. Do I stay on or do I come off?"

"Stay on, stay on," consented his overlord distractedly. "I'll get in touch with Kling about it. After all, you can only be wrong once."

They seemed to be playing craps there in the room, the way they were all down on their haunches hovering over something in the middle of the floor. You couldn't see what it was; their broad backs blotted it out completely. It was awfully small, whatever it was. Occasionally one of their hands went up and scratched at the back of its owner's rubber-tired neck in perplexity. The illusion was perfect. All that was missing was the click of bone, the lingo of the dice game.

A matron stood watchfully looking on, over by the doorway, without taking part in the proceedings herself. Something about her clashed with one's sense of fitness. Almost anyone's sense of esthetic fitness. She kidded the beholder, from the top of her head all the way down to her ankles, that she was going to end bifurcated, in a pair of trousers. Then at the ankles she ended in a skirt anyway; and the sense of harmony was revolted.

Wanger, over in the opposite doorway, where he'd just come in unnoticed, stood taking in what was going on as long as he could stand it. Finally he strode forward, the apelike conclave disintegrated, to reveal a pygmy in the middle of the giants. Cookie looked even smaller than he was against their anthropoidal bulk.

"*Not* that way, *not* that way," Wanger protested. "Whaddaya trying to do, anyway—sweat a kid that age?"

"Who's sweating him?" Wanger knew they hadn't been. One of them put away a gleaming pocket watch he'd evidently been dangling enticingly at the end of its chain with complete lack of result.

The matron threw back her head and laughed with a neigh like a horse.

Cookie, with that devilish quickness of children to scent sympathy and play up to it, took one look at Wanger, wrinkled up his muzzle into a monkey grimace and began to emit the moderator opening stanzas of a good hearty bawl.

"Yeah. See?" Wanger said, fixing an accusing eye around the

room. "Don't y'know kids that age are afraid of cops to begin with? Each one of you guys is a natural enemy to it, and when you all gang up on it at once——"

"We're in civvies, ain't we?" one of them retorted in perfect seriousness.

"He didn't see the badges, so how could he tell?"

"The expert child handler," another chuckled under his breath as they moved toward the door.

The last one said morosely, "I hope y'have better luck than we had. Jazes, I'd rather tackle the hard-to-crackest yegg any day than a kid like this that don't even know what you're saying to it at all."

"It knows all right," Wanger grunted. "It takes a little finesse, that's all."

The matron was the only one who stayed in the room, though her value was problematical. It had been found early in the game that she terrified their "material witness" far more than all the males put together. If she came any closer than the doorway, he went into nightmare hysterics.

Wanger drew up a chair, sat down on it, spread his legs at a ninety-degree angle and perched Cookie on one.

"We're going to play Charlie McCarthy again," the matron chuckled pessimistically. "I don't think he was even awake through the whole thing that night——"

"He was awake all right. Who's doing this?"

Cookie was beginning to know Wanger from previous knee "interviews." He smiled favoringly, perhaps even a trifle venally, up at him. "You got'ny more jelly beans?"

"No, the doctor says I gave y'too many already." Wanger got down to work. "Who made your daddy go in the closet, Cookie?"

"Nomebody made him, he wannedta go. He was playin' a game."

"That's the same place where y'got stumped before," the matron pointed out gratuitously.

Wanger snapped his head around with a flash of unfeigned ill temper, rare with him. "Listen, will you do me a favor!" He drew a long, preparatory belly breath to see him through what he knew he was in for. "Who was he playing the game with, Cookie?"

"Us."

"Yes, but who's us? You and who else?"

"Me and him and the lady."

"What lady?"

"The lady."

"What lady?"

"The lady that was here."

"Yes, but what lady was here?"

"The lady that—the lady that—" It wasn't that Cookie wasn't willing; the dialectics of the thing were throwing him. "The lady that was playing the game with us," he concluded with a burst of inspiration.

Wanger had nearly run through the breath supply he'd laid in by now; he let the dregs of it out with a dejected hiss.

"Y'see how he gets away from y'each time? That kid isn't going to need a mouth when he grows up."

Wanger was not in an equable mood. "Listen, McGovern, I'm not kidding, if you make one more side remark while I'm doing this——"

"Doing what?" the matron wanted to know, but with prudent inaudibility.

Wanger took out a small black pocket notebook. He turned back to his knee-riding witness, who was swinging his legs blithely. "Well, look, what was the name of the game?"

"Hide-n'-seek!" crowed Cookie positively. He was on familiar ground now.

"Whose turn was it first?"

"Mine!"

"And then whose turn was it?"

"'Nen the lady's!"

"And after that?"

"'Nen it was my daddy's turn."

"Build-up," murmured Wanger softly. He scribbled almost indecipherably on his free knee, using the curve of one arm to support his other burden: "Invegled—" He crossed it out, substituted, "Invagled—" He crossed that out, too, scrawled, "Lured in during game of hide-and-seek."

Then he looked up bitterly. "What the hell! It don't make sense! How's a strange woman that the guy never saw before going to walk into a house and get a full-grown man to play games with her—just like that!"

The sardonic matron said very softly, to make sure she couldn't be accused of having spoken at all, "You'd be surprised. But not the kind of games you mean."

The book hit the opposite wall and dropped with a little flurry.

"What'sa matter?" asked Cookie, looking after it interestedly. "What'd the book do, ha?"

"Wait a minute, you're taking it for granted he never saw her before, aren't you?" the matron tried to remind him, at the risk of her neck.

"You heard what he says each time!" Wanger hollered over at her wrathfully. "I've got it jotted down in that thing six times over! She never came to their house before."

Cookie started to pucker up into his wizened monkey expression again. "I'm not sore at you, sonny," Wanger hastily amended, patting the slope of Cookie's head mollifyingly a couple of times.

Then it suddenly came. Cookie looked up at him with the uncertainty of one whose confidence in a relationship has just been shaken. "Whoua you mad at then? Are you mad at Miss Baker?"

"Who's Miss Baker?"

"The lady that was playin' games with——"

Wanger nearly dropped him to the floor on the back of his head. "My God, I actually got her name out of him! Did you hear that? Here I didn't even think he——"

His enthusiasm was short-lived. His face dimmed again. "Aw, it was probably just a spiked handle she gave herself. She started being Miss Baker when she came in the door, she stopped being Miss Baker the minute she got outside it again. If I could only get an idea of what the stall was she sold herself to Moran on, to be let in here like that, it might help some——"

"One of the neighbors?" suggested the matron.

"We've canvassed every one of them for six blocks in all directions. Cookie, what did Miss Baker say to your daddy when he first opened the door and let her in?"

"She said hullo," he faltered tentatively, evidently doing his conscientious best to fulfil what was required of him.

"*That's* going to start in again," sighed the matron resignedly.

Wanger glanced around in the direction of the stairs. "I wonder if she'd be any help— Ask the doctor if she's in condition to come down for just a minute. Tell him I don't want to question her, y'understand, I just want to see if she can throw some light on a point the kid brought up. I won't keep her a minute."

"Don't take any lead pipe to the kid while I'm out of the room now," the matron warned. "I'm supposed to be in attendance the whole time he's with you."

She returned in a couple of minutes. "They didn't want her to, but she did want to. She'll be right down."

The doctor and a nurse both came in with her. She walked very slowly.

The murder hadn't been in the closet out there; it was in here on her face. "Now, please—" the doctor urged Wanger.

"I promise you," Wanger assured him.

She was a mother. She was half dead herself, but she was still a mother. "You're not tiring him too much, are you, officer?" She tottered over to the two of them, bent forward and kissed the youngster. The doctor and the nurse held her up, each by an arm.

Wanger almost didn't have the heart to go ahead. But, after all, it had to be done sooner or later. "Mrs. Moran, I don't suppose there's a Miss Baker that you happen to know of. . . . I'm trying to find out if there really is such a person or if it was just a . . . He just mentioned a Miss Baker——"

He saw the change come over her face before the doctor and nurse did, because she was turned toward him. It had seemed impossible a moment ago that anything could have been added to the emotion she had undergone already, and yet now something was. A climactic excess of horror, to top all the other horror she had experienced, seemed to spread slowly over her face like a cold, viscous film. She pressed two fingers to the outer edge of each eyebrow, as if to keep her skull from flying apart. "Not her!" she whispered.

"That's what he says," Wanger breathed back unwillingly.

"Oh, no—no!"

He correctly translated the meaning she gave the harried negative; not a denial of the person's existence, a denial of the accusation—simply because it was so unthinkable.

"Then there is . . ." he persisted gently.

"The child's—" She pointed, hardly able to articulate. Tears, no longer of grief but of mortal terror, welled unchecked from her eyes. "Cookie's— kindergarten teacher——"

If there was anything could make what had happened seem even worse than it was, it was this: to have the cause of it take form, materialize into human shape, cease to remain just an abstraction—become, from an impersonally barred door, the young woman who was in charge of her own child several hours each day.

She crumpled; not in a faint, but her legs gave under her. The nurse and doctor caught her, supported her between them. They pivoted her slowly around to face the door, started her over toward it, taking small steps. She was incapable of saying anything further, but nothing further needed to be said. It was all in Wanger's hands now.

Just before the door closed on the pathetic little procession, the doctor snarled crankily over his shoulder, "You fellows make me sick."

"Can't be helped," answered the detective doggedly. "Had to be done."

She was in the middle of a flock of kids in a subdivided section of the school yard, separated from the rougher activities of the older children. They were playing games, marching one at a time under the arched hands of two pivots, and then being imprisoned there and swung back and forth, and then being given a whispered choice of two incalculable treasures, and then being posted behind one or the other of the two pivots, according to the selection they'd made. They'd never played that in Wanger's day, down on East 11th Street, so he couldn't follow it very closely.

He hated to do this more than he'd ever hated any job before, even though it was not an arrest yet or anything even remotely resembling it. He supposed the sight of the kids made him feel that way. There was something brutal, almost unclean, about hauling her off from here, to find out if she had taken a human life.

She saw him watching and left them a minute and came over to him. She was a short, slender little body with coppery gold hair; young, not more than twenty-four, or -five; pretty behind her shell-rimmed glasses. In fact, even pretty before them, if a trifle more austere. Sparingly gilded with freckles on her cheekbones. They were becoming.

"Were you waiting for one of them?" she asked pleasantly. "The session won't be over for another——"

He'd asked that he be allowed to find his way out here to her unescorted—or rather guided only by a "monitor," one of the older children, who had now gone back—and hadn't explained his business to the principal; it seemed more considerate. "It's you yourself I'd like to speak to," he said. He tried to do his job without frightening her unduly. After all, she was just a stray name on a child's lips, so far. "I'm Wanger, of the police department——"

"Oh." She wasn't particularly frightened, just taken aback.

"I'd like you to come over and see Cookie Moran—you know, Mrs. Frank Moran's youngster—with me as soon as you're through here, if you don't mind."

"Ah, yes—poor little soul," she commiserated.

The game had stalled meanwhile. The children were still in playing formation, all faces turned toward her for further instructions. "Should we start pulling now, Miss Baker?"

She glanced at him inquiringly. "Finish your class out first," he consented. "I'll wait for you."

She went back to her charges immediately, no premonition of impending difficulties seeming to mar her attention to her duties. She clapped her hands briskly. "All right, now, children. Ready? Pull! . . . Not too hard now . . . Look you, Marvin, you're tearing Barbara's sleeve——"

In the classroom later, the children all safely packed into the bus and sent off, he watched her clear the desk at which she held sway over them, putting things neatly away into the drawer. "Those little crayon drawings they do for you—like those you've got there—don't they take them home every day?"

It was the idle question of a man standing by watching something he is not familiar with. It had that sound, at least.

"No, Fridays are our days for that. We let them accumulate during the week, and then on Fridays we clear out their little desks and send everything home with them to show their mothers how they're progressing." She laughed indulgently.

He picked up one of the color plates at random. It was an oversize robin perched on a limb. He chuckled with hypocritical admiration. "Is this pattern from last week or from this week?" Another of those idle, stopgap questions, as if simply to make conversation while she was straightening her hat.

"This week's," she said, glancing around to identify it. "That was their Monday afternoon assignment."

Monday night was the night——

They took a taxi to the Moran house. Wanger was the more diffident of the two, kept looking out the window on his side. "Is this a police matter you're taking me over on or, er, an errand of mercy?" she finally asked, a little embarrassedly. It wasn't the embarrassment of guilt, it was the uncertainty of a totally new, uncharted experience.

"It's just a bit of routine, don't pay any attention to it." He looked out the cab window again as though his thought were a thousand miles away. "By the way, were you over there the night it happened?" He couldn't have made it sound more inconsequential if he'd tried.

Not that he was being unduly considerate or leaning over backward about it; the situation so far didn't warrant any heavier handling. He would have been out of order.

"Over there at the Morans'?" She arched her brows in complete astonishment. "Why, good heavens, no!"

He didn't repeat the question and she didn't repeat the denial. Once each was enough. She was on record.

Wanger had looked on at many confrontations, but he thought he had never been present at a more dramatic one than this. She was so defenseless against the child, in one way. And the child was so defenseless against the whole grown-up world, in another way.

He was overjoyed to see her when the matron brought him in. "H'lo, Miss Baker!" He ran across the room to her, clasped her below the hips, looked up into her face. "I couldn't come to school today because my daddy went away. I couldn't come yesterday, either."

"I know, Cookie, we all missed you."

She turned to Wanger as if to ask, "Now what do I have to do?"

Wanger got down on his haunches, tried to keep his voice low and confidence inspiring. "Cookie, do you remember the night your daddy went into the closet?"

Cookie nodded dutifully.

"Is this the lady that was here with you in the house?" They waited.

She had to prompt him herself finally, "Was I, Cookie?"

It seemed as though he were never going to answer. The tension became almost unendurable, as far as the grown-ups in the room were concerned.

She took a deep breath, reached down, sandwiched one of his little hands between her two. "Was Miss Baker here with you the night daddy went into the closet, Cookie?" she asked.

This time the answer came so suddenly it almost jolted out of him. "Yes, Miss Baker wuss here. Miss Baker had supper with my daddy and me—'member?" But he was talking directly to her, not to them.

She straightened slowly, shaking her head blankly. "Oh, no . . . I can't understand it. . . ." Their faces had sort of closed up around her. Nothing was said.

"But, Cookie, look at me——"

"No, please don't influence him," Wanger cut in, civilly but decisively.

"I'm not trying to—" she said helplessly.

"Will you wait for me outside, Miss Baker? I'll be with you in just a moment."

When he came out presently, she was sitting by herself out there, in a chair against the wall. True, there was a man busy with something or other in one of the adjacent rooms that commanded the front door, but she didn't know that. She was fastening and unfastening the clasp of her handbag, over and over. But she looked up at him with directness. "I can't understand that——"

He didn't say anything more about it one way or the other. The child was on record now, too, that was all.

He'd brought a crayon-colored outline pattern out to show her. An oversize robin on a bough. "You've already told me that this is the pattern you gave them to fill in Monday afternoon. And that they only bring their work home once a week, on Fridays."

Her eyes clung to it much longer than was necessary for mere identification. He waited a moment, then folded it and put it away.

"But it was found right here in the house, Miss Baker, in the early hours of Tuesday morning. How do you suppose it got here?"

She just looked at the place where it had last gone into his clothing.

"It's possible, of course, that the youngster brought it home with him himself without permission that day, before it had even been marked." The suggestion came from him, questioningly.

She looked up quickly. "No, I—I don't think he did. I excused him ahead of the rest that day, because his mother was waiting outside to take him with her. You can ask Mrs. Moran, but——"

"I have already."

"Oh, well, then—" she stood up. A little added color peered slowly into her face. "Then what was that supposed to be, a verbal trap for me?"

He quirked his head noncommittally.

"This seems to have put me in a somewhat awkward position."

"Not at all," he said insincerely. "Why say that?"

She looked down at her handbag, unfastened and refastened its catch one more time, then suddenly looked up, flung at him with a spirited little flare-up of impatience that matched her hair, "Although I don't know why it should! That was hardly a fair test in there just now."

He was urbane to the point of silkiness. "Why wasn't it? Doesn't the child know you well enough? Doesn't he see you five days a week? It's not conclusive as far as we're concerned, that you're entitled to say, but fair it was."

"But don't you see? A child's mind, a child that age, is as sensitive as an exposed camera plate; it'll take the first impression that comes its way. You asked me not to influence him just now, but you men have undoubtedly already influenced him, maybe without meaning to, during the past few days. He's heard you talking about my being here and now he believes I was. In children the borderline between reality and imagination is very——"

He spoke in a patiently reasoning tone. "As far as our influencing him goes, you're entirely mistaken. We'd never heard the name, any of us, until he first mentioned it, so how could he have heard it from us first? As a matter of fact, we had to send for Mrs. Moran and have her explain who you were, when he first brought it out."

She didn't actually stamp her feet, but she gave a lunge of her body that expressed that state of mind. "But what am I supposed to have done—would you mind *telling* me? Walked out of here, when such a thing took place, without notifying anybody?"

"Now, please." He spread the flats of his hands disarmingly. "You've already told me once you weren't here, and I haven't asked you a second time, have I?"

"And I repeat I wasn't. Most decidedly! I've never been in this house before today."

"Then that's all there is to it." He made a calming motion, as of pressing something gently downward with his hands. Peace at any price. "Nothing more to be done or said about it. Just give me a rough outline of your movements that night, and we're through. You don't object, do you?"

She quieted down. "No, of course not."

"No offense, it's just routine. We've asked Mrs. Moran that herself."

She had sat down again. Quiet became thoughtfulness. "No, of course. . . ." Thoughtfulness became a loss in innermost contemplation. "No. . . ."

He cleared his throat presently. "Whenever you're ready."

"Oh, beg pardon. I seem to do everything wrong, don't I?" She opened and closed her handbag catch one final time. "The children were sent home at their usual hour. Four, that is, you know. Until I cleared my desk and so on, it must have been four-thirty by the time I left. I went back to my room at the Residence Club, stayed in it until about six, resting and doing a little personal laundering. Then I went out and had my dinner, at a little place down the block where I usually go. You want the name, I suppose?"

He looked ruefully apologetic.

"Karen Marie's; it's a little private dining room run by

a Swedish woman. Then I took a walk, and at, oh, sometime around eight, I dropped in to a moving picture——"

"Don't recall just which one it was, I suppose?" he suggested leniently, as though it were the most unimportant thing in the world.

"Oh, oh, yes. The Standard. *Mr. Smith Goes to Washington*, you know. I don't go to them very often, but when I do, the Standard's the only one I go to. Well, that's about all, I guess. I came out when the show did and got back to the Residence Club just a little before twelve."

"All right, well, that'll do very nicely. Thanks a lot, that takes care of everything. Now, I won't keep you any longer . . ."

She stood up almost unwillingly. "You know, I almost would rather not go under—under these circumstances. I'd feel better if this whole thing were cleared up one way or the other right while I'm still here."

He gave one hand a paddle twist. "There's nothing to clear up. You seem to be reading more into it than we're willing to put into it ourselves. Now don't worry about it, just run along and forget the whole business."

"Well. . . ." She went reluctantly, looking back until the very last, but she went.

The minute the front door had closed on her he seemed to get an electric shock from some unseen source. "Myers!" The man who had been in the room farther down the hall popped out. "Day and night. Don't let her out of your sight a minute." Myers went hustling by to seek the back way out.

"Brad!" Wanger called. And before the staircase had stopped swaying with tumultuous descent: "Beat it out of here fast; check with the Standard Theater and find out the name of the other picture they were showing there Monday night, with *Mr.*

Smith. That's one good thing about double features; they come in handy in our business. Then check with this Karen Marie's place; find out if she ate there, I'm going to go over this alibi of hers every inch of the way and God help her if it doesn't hold up under hundred-pound weights dropped from a height!"

First phone call to Wanger, at the Moran house, twenty minutes later:

"Hey, Lew; this is Bradford. Listen, I didn't have to check with the Standard movie house. The name of the second feature that night was *Five Little Peppers*, if you still want it. But somebody else stopped by just ahead of me and asked them the same question, I was told. The girl in the box office wondered why all the sudden interest in a grade-B filler."

"Who?" Wanger jumped through the phone at him.

"Her. The Baker girl. I got her description. Must have headed straight over there as soon as she left you. How d'ya like that?"

"I like it pretty well," answered Wanger with grim literalness. "Polish the rest of it off. The kid just came through with the color she was wearing that night. Another of those freak spills, like his popping the name. Dark blue, got it? Go over to the Residence Club, see if you can get a line of what color she had on when she left her room Monday evening; somebody might have noticed. And do it cagey; no badge. I don't want her to tumble. We're taking stitches until the sewing-up's all done. You're just a guy trying to follow up a crush on someone whose name you don't know; you can get to her by elimination."

Second phone call to Wanger, same place, half an hour later:

"Brad again. Holy smoke, is her alibi cheesecloth! I think we've got something now all right."

"All right, never mind the schoolboy ardor; when you've been at this as long as I have you'll realize that the time you think you've got the most is when you've got two big handfuls of nothing."

"Well, d'ya wanta hear it or should I keep it confidential to myself?"

"Don't get fresh, rookie. What is it?"

"She *didn't* eat in Karen Marie's that night! First the Swensky woman that runs it backed her up solid. 'Oh, ya, ya. Sure she vos dare.' Well, after what happened at that movie box office, I dunno why, but something gimme kind of a hunch, so I took a chance and played it. And it paid off! I threw a big bluff and got tough about it and told her, 'Whattaya trying to do, kid me? Don'tcha suppose I know she was just in here herself and told you to say that, if anyone asked you? Now, d'ya wanta get in trouble or d'ya wanta stay out of it?'

"She caved right in like wet cement. 'Ya,' she admitted, kind of scared, 'she vos here yust now. I like to help her if I could, but as long as you know dot already, I don't want to get in no trouble myself.'

"And wait, there's more yet. I spaded around over at the Residence Club lobby. The elevator girl and the desk clerk both remembered seeing her pass through that night, and she was wearing—dark blue."

"Come to papa," intoned Wanger fervently.

Third phone call to Wanger, next day:

"Hello, Lew? This is Myers. I'm outside the school. I've got her safely nailed down until four this afternoon. I've been practically sitting on her shoulders ever since yesterday. But here's a little something just turned up; I wanted you to get it right away. It might mean something and then again it might not. I picked her up when she came out of the Residence Club doorway just now, and on her way to the bus I noticed a fruit-stall keeper give her the old good-morning and she smiled back. So I dropped behind and cased him quick, so I'd still be able to make the same bus she did. He told me she bought half a dozen Florida oranges from him at six o'clock Monday evening. I'm remembering that two glasses of orange juice turned up in the Moran refrigerator the morning after that Mrs. Moran couldn't account for, that she was certain she didn't prepare herself before she went up to her mother's."

"I'm remembering that, too. At six she was on her way out, not in, even according to her own story. She took them somewhere with her. I'm going over there right now and have a chat with the cleaning maid that does her room. One good thing about oranges, from our point of view, is you can't eat the peel, too."

Wanger to superior:

"How's it looking up, Lew?"

"Almost too good to be true. I'm afraid to breathe on it for fear the whole thing'll collapse. Believe it or not, Chief, I've got a life-size, flesh-and-blood suspect at last, after chasing will-o'-

the-wisps until now. I've actually talked to her and heard her answer me. I keep pinching myself all the time."

"Pinch her, that'll be a little more constructive."

"This girl has tried to palm off a tissue of lies on us for an alibi. I've heard of them with one weak link, and two weak links, but this thing is spun sugar in the sun! She wasn't at the restaurant where she said she was, she wasn't at the picture show, she left her room in a dark blue outfit. The Moran kid identified her to her face as having been with him and his father that night. A crayon drawing he did in school Monday afternoon was found there in the house in the small hours of Tuesday morning, and Mrs. Moran is dead sure he didn't have it with him when she called for him and took him away. And just to do it up brown: she bought half a dozen Florida oranges at a fruit stall near the club six o'clock Monday evening and took them with her—to wherever she was going. There were two large double glasses of the stuff found standing in the Moran Frigidaire afterward that Mrs. M is positive were prepared by some other hand than her own. True, there were already oranges in her bin, to the best of her recollection. But then where did the ones this Baker girl bought go to? They never showed up in her room from first to last; I've questioned the cleaning maid and she didn't remove any orange peel from that room all week long, not so much as a dried seed.

"Now, what does it look to you?"

"It looks like three strikes and out. Suppose you let her flounder for, say, another twenty-four hours and see if she goes in any deeper. Then get ready for the jump. But don't lose her whatever you do. Stick close to her day and night——"

"And even at other times," amended Wanger remorselessly.

"This is Wanger, Chief."

"I've been waiting to hear from you. I think you better bring the Baker girl in with you now."

"I am, Chief. I'm calling you from the lobby of the Residence Club right now. I wanted your okay before I go up to her room and get her."

"All right, you've got it. I just got a report that gives the kid's story grown-up confirmation for the first time, even if it's only partial. A man named Schroeder who lives on the other side of the street a few doors down happened to go to his bedroom window to pull down the shade and definitely saw the figure of a woman leaving the Moran house shortly before midnight. He couldn't identify her at that distance and in the dark, of course, but I don't see much sense in holding off any longer."

"No, there isn't. Not with her past record of disappearances. I'll be in in about fifteen or twenty minutes."

The girl elevator operator tried to bar his way. "I'm sorry, sir, no gentlemen are allowed up in the rooms."

"I'm not a gentleman, I'm a detective," Wanger was half-tempted to say, but didn't. He had to admit there had been pickups he'd like better than this one. "The desk cleared me," he told her gruffly. She looked out across the lobby and got a surreptitious high sign that it was all right to go ahead up with him. Wanger hadn't been willing to take a chance on his slippery quarry to the extent of waiting below and having them call her down.

The girl opened for him at the seventh.

"Wait here for me. And no other passengers on the way down, straight trip."

She was all eyes as he made his way down the peaceful, homelike corridor; she could tell it was an arrest.

He knocked on the door. Her voice said unfrightenedly, "Who is it?"

"Open the door, please," he answered quietly.

She did immediately, surprise at the male voice still showing on her face. She had a washbasin full of silk stockings there behind her.

"Would you mind coming over with me?" He was somber about it but not truculent.

She said, "Oh," in a weak little voice.

He stood there waiting in the open doorway. She fumbled around for her outer things in a closet, couldn't get what she was looking for. "I don't know why I'm not frightened," she faltered. "I suppose I ought to be—" She was very badly frightened. She dropped the hanger with her coat and had to brush it off. Then she tried to put the coat on, forgetting to take the hanger out of it.

"Nothing's going to happen to you, Miss Baker," he said morosely.

"I'll have to leave my stockings go, won't I?" she said.

"I guess you better let them go."

She knitted her brows, pulled out the stopper on her way past. "I wish I'd finished them before you got here," she sighed. "Am I coming back?" she asked just before putting the lights out. "Or should I—should I take anything with me for the night?" She was very badly frightened.

He just closed the door for her.

"You see, I've never been arrested before," she said placatingly, accompanying him down the hall, quick nervous little steps to his longer slower ones.

"Cut it out, will ya?" he said gruffly, with a sort of querulous annoyance.

He came into the dim room, looked at her, lit a cigarette whose outer radius of slowly expanding smoke took a moment or two to reach the conical shaft from the shaded light over her. When it did it turned pale blue, like something in a test tube. "Crying won't do any good," he said with distant correctness. "You're not being mistreated in any way. And you have only yourself to blame for being here."

"You don't know what it means—" she said in the direction his voice had come from. "You deal in arrests, to you it's nothing. You can't possibly know what goes through you, when you're in your room, secure and contented and at peace with the world one minute, and the next someone suddenly comes for you to take you away. Takes you down through the building you live in, in front of everybody, takes you through the streets—and when they get you there you find out you're supposed to have— to have murdered a man! Oh, I can't stand it! I'm frightened of the whole world tonight! I feel as though I were in the middle of one of those stories told to my own children, suddenly come true; bewitched, held under the power of some ogre's spell."

And as she wept, she tried to smile into the darkness at them, in apology.

Another voice spoke up from the perimeter of gloom: "D'you think Moran had an easy time of it, that last half hour or so in the closet? You didn't see him when he was taken out; we did."

She pressed her hair flat to her head, soundlessly.

"Don't," Wanger said in an aside. "She's the sensitive type."

The unseen matron made a plucking sound at her lips with her tongue, to express her own opinion on that subject.

"I didn't know it was a murder. I didn't know it was done to him purposely!" the girl on the wooden chair said. "When you had me out there at their house the other day, I simply thought it had been an accident, that he'd locked himself in some way, and the child hadn't realized the seriousness of the danger, and then afterward perhaps, to escape the blame, as children will, had made up the story that I was there."

Wanger said, "That doesn't alter the case any. That's not what we're talking to you about now. You didn't eat at the Swedish woman's. You didn't go to the Standard. But you went to both of those places *afterward* and told them to say you did! Then you wonder why you're here."

She held one wrist with the other hand, twisting at it circularly. Finally she said, "I know—I didn't realize I was being watched so soon—you seemed so friendly that afternoon."

"We don't give warnings."

"I didn't know it was a murder; I thought it was just the child's little fib I had to contend with." She took a deep breath. "I was—with my husband. His name is Larry Stark, he—he lives at 420 Marcy Avenue. I made dinner for him at his apartment and was there all evening."

It made no impression. "Why didn't you tell us that the first time you were asked?"

"I couldn't, don't you see? I'm a teacher, I'm not supposed to be married, it'll cost me my job."

"We've shot your first story to pieces, there's nothing left of it; naturally you've got to replace it, you can't just stand on thin air. Why should we believe this one any more than the first?"

"Ask Larry—he'll tell you! He'll tell you I was there with him the whole time."

"We'll ask him all right. And he probably will tell us you were there with him. But the Moran child tells us you were there with *him*. And the crayon drawing tells us you were there with *him*. And the two glasses of orange juice in the icebox tell us you were there with *him*. And your dark blue suit tells us you were there with *him*. And your own actions for the past few days tell us you were there with *him*. That's quite a lineup to buck, little girl."

She gave a wordless intake of breath and let her head tilt back across the chair back.

A shaft of yellow corridor light slashed through the four-square darkness around her and a voice said, "He's ready for her now."

Wanger's chair scraped back. "It's a little late for that now. It won't do you as much good as if you'd come out with it in the beginning. This thing's well under way, Miss Baker, and it seldom pays to change trains in the middle of a trip—you're liable to fall down between the two of them."

His hand became visible up past the wrist, reaching out into the downpouring cone of light for her.

She was crying again, soundlessly as ever, when the matron and Wanger brought her up before his superior's desk.

"So this is the young lady?" Under other circumstances it might have been misconstrued as a half-friendly opening remark. It wasn't meant that way.

A phone beside him stuttered, "D-d-d-d-d-*ding*, br-r-r-r-*ring*."

He said, "Just a minute." Then he said, "Who? Yes, there's a Wanger here, but you can't use his extension. Well, what is it you——"

He lowered it, looked across the desk at him. "There's somebody has something to tell you about this girl you just brought in. Go ahead, see what it is."

He motioned, and the matron stepped outside with Miss

Baker again. "The husband, I guess," Wanger murmured, moving around beside him and picking up the instrument.

A woman's voice said, "Hello, is this Wanger?"

"Yes. Who is it wants to—" he started to say warily.

The other voice cut through his like a knife through butter. "I'm doing the talking. You've just brought a girl in with you from the Women's Residence Club. A Miss Baker, a kindergarten teacher. That right? Well, this is just to tell you she had nothing to do with what happened to Moran in that closet; I don't care how it looks or what you think you know or what you think you've found out."

Wanger started to have ants in his pants, to squirm around trying to keep the mouthpiece silenced and at the same time signal, "Trace this! Trace this!" to his superior.

The voice was almost telepathic. "Yeah, trace this, I know," it observed dryly. "I'm getting right off, so don't waste your time. Now, just in case there are any doubts in your minds, and you want to pass me off as a crank, the note pinned to the Moran kid's quilt read, 'You have a very sweet child, Mrs. Moran. I am leaving him where he will be safe until you return, as I would not want any harm to come to him for the world.' Miss Baker couldn't possibly know that, because you haven't given it out yourselves. Their radio's a Philco, he reads the *Sun*, I gave him scrambled eggs for his last meal, there were two moldy raincoats in the closet, and his whole cigar burned down without losing its shape, next to the chair he was last sitting in. You'd better let her go. Goodbye and good luck." *Click.*

The other phone on his chief's desk was ringing at that very moment. "A pay telephone in the Neumann Drugstore, corner of Dale and Twenty-third!'"

Wanger nearly pulled the door off its hinges, left it open behind him.

Six minutes and eighteen seconds later he was panting his insides out into the face of a startled proprietor hauled out from behind the prescription counter. "Who just put in a call from that middle booth there, where the bulb is still warm?"

The proprietor shrugged with expansive helplessness. "A woman. Do I know who she was?"

Wanger's record on Frank Moran:

Evidence: 1 note in hand-printed capitals pinned to quilt on child's bed.

1 crayon-colored outline drawing, probably an adult imitation of a child's handiwork.

Case Unsolved.

PART FOUR

FERGUSON

For the portent bade me understand
Some horror was at hand
       —DE MAUPASSANT

I

The Woman

IT WASN'T A well-attended exhibition, even as one-man shows go. Perhaps he hadn't made enough of a name yet. Or perhaps he had already made too much of a name—in the wrong direction. For his work was not only to be met with here, in this gallery; you could also find it on every subway newsstand in town, nearly any day in the month, hanging diagonally downward from a little clip. For twenty-five cents you could take it home with you, and get not only the cover but a whole magazine full of reading matter behind it. And that, almost anyone in attendance at the gallery would have told you, was certainly success in the wrong direction.

But there were a few who came just the same, not so much because it was his work as because it was an art exhibition. They were the usual types who never missed an art exhibition, no matter whose, no matter where. A scattering of the dilettantes, or, as they would have preferred to be known, the cognoscenti, were drifting superciliously around, simply to have something to chatter about over their next party cocktails. A stray dealer or two was on hand, just to be on the safe side if there was any interest shown in this particular talent. A couple of second-string critics were there, because of their jobs. The exhibit would get only a half column in tomorrow's papers. Encouragingly phrased, perhaps, but only a half column.

Then there were the two visiting ladies from Keokuk who had come to this because they were starting back home tomorrow night and it was the only one available in the time left to them and they had to take in at least one art exhibit while they were in the city. Anyway, his name was a nice American name, easy to remember and tell "the girls" about back home when they attended their next Ladies' Thursday.

And then there was the professional art student. You could spot her in a minute just by looking at her. Here taking notes or something. The same type that sits down and copies Old Masters in the art museums. Intensely serious, a hungry look on her face, horn-rimmed glasses, lank bobbed hair under a dowdy tam-o'-shanter, oblivious of her surroundings, moving raptly from canvas to canvas, every once in a while jotting down some mystic abracadabra of her own in a cheap little ten-cent ruled notebook.

She seemed to have some inchoate critical canons of her own; she passed by still lifes, landscapes and groups with the merest of glances. It was only the portrait heads that drew her conscientious memorandums. Or perhaps that just came under the head of specialization; she was already too far advanced in her studies for fruit and sunsets.

She crept mouselike from room to room, standing back whenever somebody wanted to get a comprehensive look at one of the same subjects she had chosen. No one even looked twice at her. To begin with, the cognoscenti were so very audible that it was hard to be aware of anyone else while they were around. They saw to that.

"Auch. His pictures are *photographs*, I tell you! It might as well be 1900. There might as well have never been Picasso. His trees are simply *trees*. They don't belong in a frame, they belong out in the woods with the other trees. What is remarkable about a tree that *looks* like a tree?"

"How right you are, Herbert! Doesn't it turn your stomach?"

"Photographs!" repeated the male cognoscente belligerently, glancing around to make sure he was overheard.

"Snapshots," contributed the female as they strode on, outraged.

One lady from Keokuk who was slightly hard of hearing asked her companion, "What're they mad at, Grace?"

"They're mad because you can recognize what the pictures are about," the other one whispered informatively.

The art student sidled inconspicuously by, without pausing before the scorned trees—which should have been shriveled and sere by now, after the blast they'd received.

The cognoscenti had stopped and taken out their scalpels again, this time before a portrait.

"Isn't that too pathetic for words? He shows the part in her hair, the very shadow cast by her lower lip. Why bother doing a picture at all? Why doesn't he just take a living girl and stand her up there behind an empty frame? *Realism!*"

"Or why not just hang up a mirror and call it *Portrait of the Passerby? Naturalism!* Bah!"

The art student came up in their wake and this time jotted down a note. Or rather, a pothook. The little lined blank book she was carrying bore four scribbled notations: "Black," "blond," "red" and "intermediate." Under "black" was a long perpendicular column of pothooks. Under "blond" there were only two. Under the other two classifications none at all, so far. She was evidently spending her afternoon taking a census of the types of hair coloration to be found in a cross section of this particular exhibitor! Strange are the ways of art students.

The gallery was closing for the afternoon now. The stray dealer or two had gone long ago; there was nothing here for them. Good enough stuff, but why load up on it? The few-remaining bitter-enders came straggling out. The cognoscenti emerged, still loudly complaining. "What a waste of time! I told you we should have gone to see that new foreign film instead." It was noticeable, however, that they had remained as long as there was anyone at all around to hear their pontifications.

The visiting ladies from Keokuk came out with a grim air of having done their duty. "Well, we kept our word," one consoled the other. "It's sure hard on your feet though, isn't it?"

The art student was the last one of all to leave. The notations in her little blank book now stood: black—15; blond—2; red—0; intermediate—1. Out of a total of eighteen portrait heads he had displayed, one conclusion was possible: the artist had a penchant for dark-haired subjects.

At any rate, she alone of all the visitors had an air of having put in a thoroughly satisfactory afternoon, of having accomplished just what she had set out to do.

She buttoned her shabby coat close up under her chin and trudged up the darkening street, back into the anonymity from which she had emerged.

II

Ferguson

FERGUSON HAD JUST finished arranging his easel and canvas when the knock on the door came. "Be right with you," he said, and started laying out his oil tubes.

He didn't look like a painter. Maybe because they don't anymore. He didn't have a beard, or a beret, or a smock, or velvet pants. He knocked down a thousand a magazine cover. But in between he liked to do serious stuff, "for himself," as he put it. One whole side of the studio was glass—the essential northern light. But that side didn't rise up straight like the other three walls; it slanted in at an angle, so that it was a cross between an upright wall and a skylight.

He went over to the door and opened it. "You the new model?" he said. "Come over here by the light and let me look at you. I don't know whether I can use you or not. I told the agency I wanted a——"

He stopped faultfinding and held his breath. He had her over in the full glare of the skylight wall by now. "Sa-ay," he exhaled finally, between a long-drawn whistle and reverent hiss. "Where have you been keeping yourself? Turn around a little, that's it. Maybe you don't fit the specifications for the ginger-ale spread, but, baby, I'm using you all right! You're just what I had in mind for that Diana-the-huntress thing, for myself. I think I'll begin that, now that you're here, and the commercial can wait."

She was raven haired, creamy skinned, and her eyes seemed violet behind the imperceptible shadow line she had drawn around them.

"Who'd you work for last?"

"Terry Kaufmann."

"What's he trying to do, hog you all to himself?"

"Do you know him?" she asked.

"Sure I know the bum," he said jocularly.

She dropped her eyes momentarily, caught her lip between her teeth.

Then she looked up at him with renewed confidence.

He was rubbing his hands exuberantly, overjoyed at this unexpected find. "Now, there could be only one possible catch. How's the figure?"

"Okay, I guess," she said demurely.

"Y'better let me see for myself. You can go in the dressing room there and hang up your things. You'll find the stuff I want you to put on all laid out in there. The gold bangle goes on the left arm, and hook the leopard-skin kilt so that the opening's at the side; your thigh shows through."

She moistened her lips. One hand went helplessly up toward her shoulder. "Is that all?"

"That's all; it's a semi-nude. Why? You've posed before, haven't you?"

"Yes," she said, face impassive, and went unhesitatingly into the dressing room.

She came out again, as unhesitatingly, but with her face held rigidly half-averted, in about five minutes' time. Her bare feet made no sound on the floor.

"Beautiful!" he said fervently. "Too bad those things don't last. In two years it'll be gone, as soon as they start dragging you around to cocktail parties. What's your name?"

"Christine Bell." she said.

"All right, now get up there and I'll show you how I want you. It's going to be a very tough pose to hold, but we'll take it in easy shifts. Crouch forward now, dead center toward the canvas, one leg out behind you. I want her to seem to be coming right out of the frame at them when they look at the picture. Right arm bent out in front of you, grasping something, like this. Left arm drawn back, past your shoulder. That's it. *Freeze.* Steady, now, steady. You're supposed to be stalking something, about to let fly an arrow at it. I'll put the bow in later; you ob viously couldn't pose for any length of time holding it stretched taut, the strain would be unendurable."

He didn't speak anymore once he had begun to work. At the end of thirty minutes she moaned slightly. "All right, let's knock off for five minutes," he said casually. He picked up a crumpled package of cigarettes, took one out, tossed the package lightly over to her on the stand.

She let it fall to the floor. Her face was white with anguish when he turned to look at her. His eyes narrowed speculatively. "Are you as experienced as you say?"

"Oh, yes, I——"

Before she could go ahead there was a sudden knock at the door. "Busy working, come back later," he called. The knock repeated itself. The girl on the stand made a supplicating gesture, said hurriedly, "Mr. Ferguson, I need the money so bad;

give me a chance, won't you? That's probably the model from the agency——"

"Then what are you doing here?"

"I was hanging around there trying to get taken on, but they won't take you on, they've got a waiting list this long, and I heard them telephoning to her to report over here to you, so I went downstairs and called her back from a public booth and let her think it was still the agency. I told her it was an error, she wasn't wanted after all, and I came over in her place; but I guess she's found out since. Won't you try me at least, won't I do?" The pleading look on her face would have melted a heart of stone, much less an artist's susceptible one, always touched by beauty.

"Tell you better in a minute." He seemed to be having a hard time keeping a straight face. "Get back out of sight," he whispered conspiratorially. "We'll give it the old Judgment-of-Paris workout."

He went to the door, held it open narrowly, staring intently outside with critical appraisal. Once he turned his head and glanced over at the first candidate, cowering against the wall, arms crossed over her bosom with unconscious—or *was* it unconscious—artistry. Then he reached into his pocket, took out a crumpled bill, handed it through the door. "Here's your carfare, kid; I won't need you," he said gruffly.

He went back to the easel with a suppressed grin struggling to free itself at the corners of his mouth. "There's even muscling-in in *this* racket," he chuckled. The grin overspread his features unhampered. "Okay, Diana, up and at 'em!"

He poised his brush again.

Corey, highball glass in hand, paused before the easel in the course of his aimless wandering about the studio, fingered the burlap carelessly flung over it. "What's this, the latest master-piece? Mind if I take a look?"

"No, stay away from that. I don't like anyone to see my pieces before they're finished," Ferguson answered above the hiss of the seltzer water.

"You don't have to be bashful with me, I'm not a competitor. What I don't know about art would—" The sacking had gone up and he was standing there rooted to the spot.

Ferguson turned his head at the continuing silence. "Well, if it takes your breath away like that before it's even finished," he said hopefully, "imagine what it'll do after the fixative's gone on."

Corey shook his head vaguely. "No, I'm trying to think. There's something vaguely familiar about that girl's face."

"Oh, sure, I expected that," Ferguson said dryly. "Well, you don't get her phone number out of me, not till after this picture's finished, if that's what you're—"

"No, I mean it. It hit me like a flash when I first lifted the sacking. Now I've lost it again. Like when you have a word on the tip of your tongue and can't bring it out. *Where* the devil have I seen those ice-cold eyes before and that warm, kissable mouth? What's her name?"

"Christine Bell."

"I don't know her by name, at any rate. Have you ever used her before? Maybe I've seen her on some of your covers."

"No, she's brand-new. I'm just breaking her in, so you haven't."

"There's just enough familiarity about the eyes and mouth to tease my memory. There isn't enough about the whole head in general, the hair for instance, to help me place her definitely. Damn it, Ferg, I *know* I've seen that girl somewhere before!"

Ferguson dropped the protective sacking over the canvas once more, somewhat like a jealous hen guarding its chick. They both moved away.

But Corey came back to the subject again later, just before he left, as though it had lain uppermost in his mind all the while. "I won't get any sleep now until I get straightened out on that." He went out, casting troubled backward glances at the covered canvas to the very last, until the door had closed after him.

She winced delicately as Ferguson notched the arrow into the bowstring, fitted the integrated weapon into the formalized pose of her hands. "Wasn't that *horrible*, the way that snapped through my fingers yesterday? I almost hate to touch it, after that!"

He laughed good-naturedly. "It wasn't horrible, but it sure could have been—if my neck had been two inches farther back, where it belonged and where it had been a minute before! What saved me was I happened to bend my head toward the canvas just then to concentrate on a detail I was working on. I felt this streak of air shoot past the nape of my neck and the next thing I knew the arrow was wobbling in the wooden frame between two of the skylight panes over there."

"But it could have killed you, couldn't it?" she lamented, wide-eyed.

"If it had happened to hit me in the right place—the jugular vein or dead center to the heart—I suppose so. But it didn't, so why worry about it?"

"But wouldn't it be better if I used one with a guard, a protective knob on the end of it?"

"No, no, I'm nothing if not realistic; I go flat when I fake things, even such a simple thing as an arrowhead. Don't be nervous now. It was just one of those hundred-to-one shots. Most likely you were unconsciously pulling it tighter and tighter as the tension of posing grew on you, and then without realizing it you let your muscles relax to try to ease them, and the damn thing sprang! Just remember not to pull it all the way back. Pull it only enough so that the bowstring isn't relaxed, forms a straight line to the arrow cleft; that's all you've got to do."

When they had taken time out and the cigarette package had passed between them on the fly, as a hand cloth does between gymnasts, she remarked, "Strange that you should become a painter."

"Why?"

"You always think of them as sort of gentle people. At least, I always did until now."

"I am gentle. What makes you think I'm not?"

She murmured, so low he could barely hear her, "Maybe you are now. You weren't always so gentle."

Then afterward, when she was back on the stand, bow stretched toward him in shooting position, she said, "Ferguson, you bring happiness to many people. Did you ever—bring death to anyone?"

His brush halted in midair, but he didn't turn to look at her. He stared before him as though seeing something in the past. "Yes, I have," he said in a subdued voice. His head inclined a little. Then he straightened it, went ahead retouching. "Don't talk to me while I'm working," he reminded her evenly.

She didn't anymore, after that. There wasn't a sound in the studio, and scarcely a motion. Only two things moved; the long slender stem of the paintbrush between his deft fingers; the retreating steel-tipped head of the arrow as it slipped slowly back upon the shaft to the position of uttermost tension the cord was capable of. A third thing there was that moved: a shadow played back and forth across the hollow of her left arm, as the white flesh contracted, as the tendons below it strained. Only those three things were not still, in the vibrant, supercharged silence.

Then suddenly there was a rain of jovial blows against the studio door, and a bevy of voices called, "Come on, Ferg, let us in. Union hours, you know!"

The arrowhead edged unnoticeably forward again, past the staff, as the strain was let out of the cord, degree by degree. She exhaled in such a peculiar, exhausted way that he turned to ask, "Matter, can't you take it?"

She shrugged, threw him a glazed smile, "Sure, but—too bad we couldn't have finished it, while we were at it."

She had never dressed under such difficulties before. The dressing-room door had no lock, and after the first inadvertent discovery that she was in there, they kept purposely trying to break in on her every few minutes, to tease her. Even Ferguson added his voice to the good-natured clamor. "Come on out, Diana, don't be modest—you're among friends."

Once the critical moment of transition from the leopard kilt to nothing to her own underthings was safely past, the worst was over. She effected this by wedging herself against the door—it opened inward—and blocking it with her body while she struggled into her things. Every moment or two it flounced against her, forcing her forward a little; then she would flatten it behind her again and go ahead with her dressing. She had never put on stockings that way before; it was an acrobatic feat.

Judging from the sounds going on in the studio proper, the party was no temporary intrusion. It was going to be an all-night affair, one of those snowball things that kept rolling up more people as it went along. Twice already the outer door had stormed open and new voices had come screaming in. "So this is where you are! I went looking for you at Mario's and when you weren't there——"

Once she heard Ferguson at the phone bawling his lungs out above the bedlam: "Hello, Tony? Send over some one-gallon jugs of Spanish red. That monthly hurricane has just hit here again. Yeah, you know the one."

There were shrieks of protest, "What that man makes on commercials alone, and the best he can offer us is Spanish red!"

"Champagne! Champagne! Champagne, or we'll all go home!"

"All right, go home!"

"Just for that we won't! Ble-e-eh."

Dressed, she stroked the side of her own face uncertainly, looked around. There was no other way out of here than through the studio. She turned, opened the door narrowly and peered out. They were already thick as bees out there—or seemed to be, the restless way they kept moiling around. Somebody had brought in some sort of stringed instrument—as bohemians, they evidently wanted no part of mechanical music—and was plucking vigorously if not too expertly at it. A girl was dancing on the model's platform.

She watched her chance, and when the line of escape from dressing room to studio door was least populous, she slipped out, threaded her way diagonally across that corner of the vast room and tried to make her exit unobserved—or at least unquestioned.

It was an attempt that was foredoomed to failure. Somebody shouted, "Look, Diana!" There was a concerted rush over toward her, and she was swept into their midst as if by a maelstrom. They were unhampered by conventional formality.

"How beautiful! Oh, just look, how beautiful!"

"And trembling like a frightened gazelle. Ah, Sonya, why don't you tremble for me like that anymore?"

"I do darling, I still do; but with laughter now, every time I look at you."

When the first effusion of appraisal and praise was over, she managed to draw Ferguson aside. "I have to go——"

"But why?"

"I don't want all these people to—to see me—I'm not used to it——"

He misunderstood. "On account of the picture, you mean? Because it's a semi-nude?" He found this so charming, he promptly repeated it to the whole assemblage at the top of his voice.

They found it charming, too; it was that thing they were always looking for, the unusual. This brought on another group formation around her. The girl named Sonya seized her hand, clasped it protectively between her two, blew upon it as if to cherish some impalpable virtue it possessed. "Ah, she's still so innocent!" she condoled, no sarcasm intended. "Never mind, dear. Just spend ten minutes in my Gil's company and you'll get over it."

"Did *you?*" somebody asked her.

"No," she shrugged. "He spent five minutes in *my* company and *he* got it."

They meant well. Ferguson backed the canvas to the wall. "Nobody look at that picture. Nobody so much as *think* about it!"

"She ends below the shoulders!" somebody else proclaimed.

"She is a bust," Sonya added fervently. Then with a quick clutch at her arm, "Not in the slang sense, dear."

If her unease had stemmed from the cause they ascribed it to, she could not have helped but overcome it; they all tried so heartily to make her feel at home. Since it didn't, it persisted. She finally acquiesced to the extent of sitting on the floor against the far wall, a cup of untasted red wine on one side of her, an intense young man reciting some of his own blank verse on the other. She sat there passively, but her eyes kept calculatingly measuring the distance between herself and the studio door. Her hands suddenly clenched spasmodically on the floor, slowly opened out again.

"Ah!" the blank-verse poet exulted. "That last line struck home. Its beauty pierced your heart. I could tell by the change that came over your face."

He was wrong.

Corey had just turned up across the room from her, was standing there over by the entrance—drawn as unerringly by a party, any party, even one going on all the way across town from him, as a bloodhound is by the scent he has been set to track down.

Seconds hung like moments in the air, moments hung like quarter hours. Her eyes, which had sought refuge on the floor, slowly, unwillingly traveled the ascending arc of the figure that had come to halt directly before her.

"Wait, let him finish first," she had said in a smothered voice. The intense young man's blank verse had never been as highly appreciated before as at this moment, would never be again.

Thick soles with welt edges. Heavy brown brogues with punctured scrollwork on their toes. Ten-dollar shoes. Then long legs, in trousers of a fuzzy tweed mixture. The hands—they'd tell, wouldn't they? Still unflexed. One hooked onto a side coat pocket by its thumb, the other negligently holding a cigarette just a little above hip level. Signet ring on its little finger. Golden glint of hair on its back, visible only by indirection. Two-button jacket, top one left open. The face was coming, couldn't be dodged any longer. The tie, the collar, the chin. The face at last. The two looks, fusing just as the last line of blank verse died into silence.

Then Ferguson's jovial voice, somewhere close beside them: "Now call his bluff, Diana!"

She got up slowly, at bay against the wall, working her back against it a little to aid her legs. "I can't," she said to where the voice had come from, without looking that way, "until you tell me what it is—and until you introduce me."

"There you are, there's your answer!" Ferguson jeered at him.

Corey wouldn't take his eyes off her. She couldn't take hers off him, as though afraid to trust him out of their sight a single instant. He said, "All kidding aside, haven't I met you before?"

Even if she'd given an answer, even if she'd wanted to, it would have been drowned in the howl of friendly derision that went up.

"Look, there are moths flying around from that one!"

"You should oil up that technique."

"Is that the best the Great Lover can get off?"

Sonya squalled informatively to someone, with that dead-earnest mannerism of hers, "Yes, didn't you know? That's how they make girls in the upper-middle classes. A friend of mine who went uptown once told me. She had it said to her three times in one night."

Corey was laughing with them at his own expense, shoulders shaking, facial muscles working, everything humorously attuned except those coldly speculative eyes that wouldn't leave hers.

The girl they held pressed to the wall with their stabbing stare shook her head slightly, smiled a little in regretful negation. She stood there a moment, then maneuvered her way out of the corner pocket he had her backed into, sauntered across the room, conscious his head had turned to look after her, conscious his eyes were following her every aimless step of the way.

She found refuge on the other side of the studio for a while, took shelter with almost the entire personnel of the party between them for a buffer. In fifteen minutes he had marked her down again, came bringing a cup of red wine over, for an excuse.

She seemed to grow rigid when she saw what he was bringing her, swallowed hard, as though there lay some danger in the imminent courtesy itself, apart from the fact of his approach.

He reached her finally, held it out to her, and the pupils of her eyes dilated. She seemed afraid to accept it and equally afraid to refuse it, afraid to drink it and equally afraid to set it aside untasted—as though anything she did with it bore a penalty of flashing recollection. She took it finally, touched it toward her lips, then held it behind her with one hand, safely out of sight.

He said, blinking troubledly, "I nearly had it for a minute when I handed you that just then, and then I lost it again."

"You're torturing the hell out of me, quit it!" she flared with unexpected savagery. She turned away from him and went into the dressing room.

He followed her even in there after a decent interval of ten minutes or so. There was no impropriety in it, the room was open to the party now.

She began busily tapping at her nose with a puff before the

mirror the instant that she saw him nearing the outside of the doorway. Until then—

He came up behind her. She saw him in the glass but didn't seem to. Standing at her shoulder he placed his hands one at each side of her face, as if trying to obliterate the dark luxuriant masses of hair that framed it.

She stood motionless under the ministration, without breathing. "What're you doing that for?" She didn't pretend to misunderstand it as a caress.

He sighed and his hands fell away. He hadn't been able to cover her entire head with them after all.

She turned partly aside from him, folded her arms, chafed their upper parts uncomfortably, bent her head downward. It was a pose strangely suggestive of penitence. She wasn't thinking in terms of penitence. She was seeing in her mind's eye a sharp little paint-scraping knife of Ferguson's that was somewhere about the place. She was seeing in her mind's eye the masses of people there were in the adjoining room. Perhaps, too, the diagonal line of escape that led from this dressing room to the outside studio door.

He'd finished lighting a cigarette. He spoke through smoke. "It wouldn't bother me like this if it weren't so."

"It isn't so," she said dully. With dangerous dullness, still looking down.

"I'll get it eventually. It'll suddenly come to me when I least expect it. Maybe five minutes from now. Maybe later on tonight, before the party's over. Maybe not for days. What's the matter? You're looking a little pale."

"It's so stuffy in here. And that red wine, I'm not used to it—especially on an empty stomach, you know."

"You haven't eaten?" he said with extravagant concern.

"No, I was posing, you know, when they broke in on us, and I haven't been able to get away since. *He* doesn't seem to feel it, but I haven't had anything since ten this morning."

"Well, er, how about coming out and having something with me now? Even though I don't exactly seem to have made a hit——"

"Why shouldn't I go with you? I have nothing against you. All contributions gratefully accepted."

"Don't say anything to the rest of them or they'll gang up on us."

"No," she agreed, "it would be better if we're not seen leaving——"

"Have you got everything? I had a hat out there somewhere in that pile. I'll see if I can dredge it up on the Q.T. Meet me over by the door; we'll make a break and run for it."

Their crafty preparations for impending departure did not go as unnoticed as they had hoped. Sonya chugged past at random, trailing clouds of cigarette smoke after her like a straining locomotive on an upgrade.

"Watch yourself with him," she said curtly over her shoulder.

The overshadowed figure behind her murmured with a gleam of eyes, "I'll make sure he doesn't get very far past just telling me where it is he thinks he saw me before."

"And just in case your hands slip off the throttle, here—take down my address. You can come around and have a nice long cry at my place tomorrow. There's nothing like a good stiff cry for washing down a seduction. And I'll make you some of my own special borscht."

"I'll watch out."

Sonya wasn't being flippant, far from it. "No, the reason I warn you is he's got such a direct approach that no one ever takes it seriously—until it's over. A girl I used to go around with—she laughed her head off at him all night long at a party one night. She only let him take her as far as her door. Then the next day she came around and ate borscht."

She went chugging off again billowing plumes of smoke. You almost expected to hear a train whistle blow.

They'd got as far as the foot of the outside stairs when they were stopped again. There was a thundering stampede behind them that sounded like six people in pursuit. It was only Ferguson.

"Say, will you do your foraging someplace else? I need her for a picture."

"Do you own her soul?"

"Yes!"

"Fine. Well, then, it's just the body I'm taking with me. You'll find her soul up there on the canvas."

Ferguson straightened his tie determinedly. "Well, then, we're both going with the body."

They weren't openly truculent about it, but both were in that mercurial state of mind where there is no longer much of a borderline between horseplay and hostility.

The girl surreptitiously sliced her hand against the side of Corey's arm, as if asking him to leave this to her, drew Ferguson a few steps away, out of earshot.

"I'm going with him—*to get rid of him.* This is the simplest way there is. See if you can clear the rest of them out up there; I'll come back later and we'll finish the picture. Or have you had too much to drink?"

"This red ink? This isn't drink."

"Well, don't drink any more then. I'll be back in an hour—in an hour and a half at the latest. Be sure you have them out by then. Wait up there for me."

"Is that a promise?"

"That's more than a promise, it's a dedication."

He turned and, without another word, tramped stolidly up the stairs.

Corey prodded a wall switch, and a small apartment living room lit up. "After you," he said with mock gallantry.

She took two bored steps forward into the place and let her eyes stray halfheartedly around, without any real interest. "Well, now what do we do here?" she asked abruptly.

He shied his hat off someplace where there was nothing to catch it. "You don't seem to get the hang of things very easily, do you?" he said, thin lipped with annoyance. "Do you have to have outline drawings?"

She turned her face aside to her shoulder an instant. "Don't. I hate that word."

She moved ahead toward a dark opening. "What's in there?"

"The other room," he said disgruntledly. "Go ahead in and see it by yourself if you want to. I'm warning you, you're rushing things. That doesn't come for about another ten minutes yet."

It lighted up and she passed from sight. It darkened and she came in again to where he was. He was swirling a coil of rye around in the bottom of a glass. "Aren't you terrified?" he sneered. "It was a bedroom!"

A scornful catch sounded in her throat. "You're the one seems to be terrified. What do you have to do, build up your courage with that stuff?"

"We'll take that up in a few minutes—if you've got breath enough left to ask it."

She went over to a kneehole desk, shot open a drawer or two. "Desk," he said scathingly. "You know, four legs, something you write on." He put his glass down. "Lemme get something straight, just for the record. What was *your* idea was going to happen when you okayed coming up here with me? You were willing enough when I first put it up to you."

"Because you were too willing to see me back to my place otherwise. My willingness beat yours to the punch, that was all."

"And what's over at your place that you're leery of?"

She shot open a third drawer, shot it closed again. "You name it. My dear old mother. A six-month-old kid that I support by my modeling. Or maybe it's just that the washbasin is cracked."

He loosened his collar so abruptly the button flew off. "Well, the hell with your background, I'm going to give you a future. This is the works—now."

She shot open a fourth drawer, looked down, smiled a little. "I knew there was one someplace around here. I saw a box of the cartridges in the bureau drawer inside." She came up with an automatic.

He kept coming on over, necktie cockeyed. "Put that down! D'ya want to have an accident?"

"I don't have accidents," she murmured placidly. She measured the weapon lengthwise in the flat of one hand, thumbed the trigger.

"It's loaded, you damn nitwit!"

"Then don't try jerking it away from me, that's what always sets them off. The safety's down now, too." She laid it down on the desk before her, but without taking her finger out of the trigger scabbard. He was in a state of mind where an antiaircraft gun wouldn't have been able to do much with him. He caught her from behind in a double-furled embrace and hid her face under his own. Her hand stayed motionless on the desk, hooked in the gun, the whole time.

His face got out of the way finally—he had to breathe himself—and hers came into view again.

She drew her free hand across it with a grimace that wasn't calculated to do his ego any good. "Don't kiss me, you fool. I'm not out for love."

"What are you out for then?"

"Nothing—as far as you're concerned. You have nothing that I want, you have nothing that—is coming to me."

Her attitude shriveled him like a June bug in a match flame. He rammed his hands into his pockets with force enough to drive them in almost up to his elbows.

The gun slid off the desk top, and she sauntered casually over toward the outside door, with it dangling from her one hooked finger.

"Come back here with that. Where do you think you're going with it?"

"Only as far as the front door. I don't know anything about you. I want to be sure that I get out of here. I'll leave it just inside the doorsill."

His voice shook with masculine outrage. "Go ahead if you want to go that badly. I'm not that hard up."

He heard the door open, and when he took a quick step out into the little entryway, the gun was lying there mockingly on the threshold. He could hear her going down the stairs—but with deliberation, not with hate. Even that concession to his injured self-esteem was lacking.

"I'll get who you are yet!" he called down after her wrathfully.

Her answer came back from a floor below. "Better be thankful that you haven't."

The walloping slam he gave his door stunned the house like a shrapnel explosion. He picked up his empty whiskey glass and smashed it all the way across the room. He picked up a pottery ashtray and smashed that, too.

He called her every name under the sun but murderer; he didn't happen to think of that one.

He called her every name but the right one.

Less than an hour later the light flashed on in the pitch-black bedroom with explosive suddenness, like a flashlight photograph, revealing Corey in blazer-striped pajamas, lying in a trough of tortured bed coverings, hand outstretched to the switch of the bedside lamp. He squinted protectively, unable to bear the brightness after the long hours of lying there in the dark. His hair was a briery mass that bespoke repeated digital massaging. A pyramid of cigarette butts topped the tray next to him, and he added one last one to the accumulation with a triumphant downward stab that showed it had finally brought results. "Damn it, I knew I'd seen her someplace be—" he muttered disjointedly.

The clock said 3:20.

Then, as the implications of the discovery hit him fully, his eyes opened to their full extent and he swung his legs to the floor. "The girl that was with Bliss that night! She's already killed a man! I'm going to warn him right now to look out!"

He pounded outside in bare feet, came back again bringing the telephone directory from the hall, sat down on the bed with it, ran his finger down the column of *F*'s, stopped at Ferguson.

Then he looked at the clock again; 3:23. "He'll think I'm nuts," he murmured undecidedly. "The first thing in the morning'll be time enough. I wonder if it really *is* the same girl; the other one was yellow as a buttercup, this one's dark as a raven."

Then, with a renewed stiffening of resolution, "I was never yet wrong in my life about a thing like this. He's got to be told, I don't care what time of night it is!" He flung the directory aside, barefooted it back to the hall and began dialing the number of Fergusons studio.

The call signal at the other end went on interminably; no one came to the phone to answer. He hung up finally, massaged his hair a couple more times. The party must be over by this time. Maybe Ferguson didn't sleep there in the studio at nights. Sure he did, he must; Corey remembered seeing a bed in one of the rooms.

Well, he'd gone on someplace else then with the rest of them. It would have to wait until morning. He got back in bed, snapped out the light.

Two minutes later it had flashed on again, and he was struggling into his trousers. "I don't know why I'm doing this," he tried to reason with himself, "but I can't sleep until I get in touch with that guy." He shrugged on his coat, spliced the two ends of his necktie in a sketchy knot, closed the door after him. He went downstairs, drummed up a cab, gave Ferguson's address. Rationally, there was no basis whatever for his behavior, he had to admit. He was going to be made the laughingstock of everyone who knew him; their kindest explanation would be that he was drunk and suffering a mild case of the D.T.'s. Chasing down in the middle of the night to tell a guy, "Look out, your model's going to kill you!" But he was in the grip of something irrational; he couldn't explain what it was himself. A hunch, a premonition, a sense of impending danger. If Ferguson was out, he'd leave a note under the door: "She's the girl who was with Bliss the night he died, I remember now. Keep your eye on her." At least give the guy a chance to defend himself.

A knock at the studio door, when he stood before it presently, brought no more results than the phone call had. He noticed something that confirmed his hunch: Ferguson not only worked here but lived here, as well. A small thing, a slight thing—an empty milk bottle standing to one side of the door.

That finished it. Milk bottles are not put out before you go, but after you come back. He was in there, he was almost certainly in there. Corey had a premonition of doom now that wouldn't be dispelled.

He went downstairs and roused the building superintendent, unconcerned at the wrathful reception that greeted him.

"Yeah, he sleeps up there in the studio. But he might be out. Them artist fellows are up all night sometimes. What's all the excitement for?"

"You open that door for me," Corey panted in a voice that brooked no argument. "I'll take the responsibility if I'm wrong. But I'm not getting out of here until you come up and open that door for me, understand?"

The super grumblingly preceded him up the stairs, jangled keys, knocked uselessly before fitting one to the door. Corey knew where the switch was, reached around him backhand and plugged it on. The two of them stood there looking down the long vista of light to the far end where the black skylight panes slanted down and the outside night began.

All Corey said, in a strangely anticlimactic, almost subdued voice, was, "I knew it."

Ferguson was lying facedown before the easel. The wicked steel sliver of the arrowhead protruded from his back, over the heart, forced through by the fall itself to that additional penetration. In front, when they turned him over, the feathered end of it had been splintered by the fall, was at right angles to the rest of the shaft. He must have turned full face toward the stand at the instant it winged at him to receive it dead center to the heart like that.

Above him brooded Diana the huntress, Diana the killer—faceless now. The features that had tormented Corey were gone. An oval hole in the canvas, cut by a paint-scraping knife, occupied their place. The bow, cord slack now, balanced mockingly across one corner of the modeling stand.

Corey brooded, "I didn't tumble in time, she beat me to it. He must have posed her late at night, to finish it up."

"What d'ya suppose it was?" the super breathed, awestruck, after they'd put in the call and stood there in the open doorway, waiting for the police. "Her grip on the bowstring accidentally slipped and the arrow flew out?"

"No," Corey murmured. "No. Diana the huntress came to life."

III

Postmortem on Ferguson

"AND THEN SHE moved over here like this." Corey was warming up to his reenactment as he went along, as any good actor does when he has a sympathetic audience and is enjoying his role. A cigarette hanging from the corner of his mouth vibrated with animation whenever he spoke. He was in his shirt sleeves, vest unbuttoned. A string of hair had come down over his forehead with the ardor of his movements.

"Go on," Wanger nodded.

"Then she starts casing the drawers one by one like this, slap—slap—slap. Hell, I didn't get it. I figured she was just stalling, giving herself something to do with her hands, you know; killing time like they do until the clinch caught up with her. So then she hits the one it's in and comes up with it——"

"Wait a minute, wait a minute—" Wanger started from his chair, made a hasty gesture of dissuasion. "Don't touch it. We may still be able to get her prints off it. Have you handled it much yourself since she picked it up?"

Corey's arrested hand hung like a claw over it. "No, only to put it back in. But I haven't finished telling you what she did with it afterward——"

"All right, but first let me wrap it up. I want to have it checked—with your permission."

"Help yourself." He stood aside while Wanger took out a handkerchief, dipped into the drawer with it and transferred it to his pocket.

"I'll see that you get it back," Wanger promised.

"No hurry. Only too glad to be of some help." The performance resumed. "So then, she doodles around with it. I go over and give her the old branding iron and—" he looked genuinely outraged all over again, even though this was only a recapitulation "—and it didn't take."

Wanger nodded with masculine understanding. "She wasn't having any."

"She wasn't having any. She says, 'I don't want love, I don't want kisses,' and she goes over to the door, gun and all. I follow her, and she's left it lying there inside the sill, and she's already halfway down the stairs. So I called down after her that I'd figure out who she was if it took me all the rest of the night, and she calls up to me, 'Better be thankful you haven't.'"

He got white around the mouth with virtuous indignation. "The little so-and-so, I'd like to give her a biff across the snout! I don't mind a jane standing you off as long as she's scared about it. But one thing gripes me is a jane standing you off and being fresh about it at the same time!"

Wanger could see his point perfectly. He'd been led on for some reason best known to herself by the murderous little trickster and then dished out of what he had a right to expect was coming to him. As far as Wanger's personal feelings entered into it—and they didn't at all—he liked this guy.

He drummed nails on the chair arm. "As I see it, there are three possible explanations for her coming up here with you like she did, before going back and killing the guy she had in mind to all along. One, she intended getting rid of you first, before you had a chance to warn Ferguson and throw a monkey wrench into the main business at hand. After she got here with you, you still hadn't remembered who she was, so she changed her mind; she'd got you away from the party, and that was the most important thing. She figured she'd have time enough to get back there and finish up before it finally dawned on you where you'd seen her before. Two, she came up only to get the weapon and use it on him. No, that won't hold up. My brain's hitting on two cylinders. She left it behind her, inside the door. Well, three is you were pestering her at the party and she was afraid you would stay on after the others and gum the works up, so she took the easiest way of eliminating you. Gave you a tease treatment and then left you flat."

Corey looked as though this last suggestion didn't do his self-esteem any too much good, but he swallowed it.

"I think a combination of one and three is as close as we can get to it at the first sitting," Wanger went on, getting ready to leave. "She came up here with you because you were getting in her hair. She intended giving you the gun if you came through with who she was, but if you didn't, she was going to let you go. You didn't, and she let you go. Come in tomorrow, will you? I want to go over the whole thing with you again. Just ask for me, Wanger's the name."

Day was breaking when he got back to headquarters, and daybreak wasn't lovely around headquarters, inside or out. He was tired, and it was the hour when human vitality is at its lowest. He went into his superior's untenanted office, slumped into a chair at the desk and let his head plop into his pronged fingers. "Why the hell did that woman have to be born?" he groaned softly. After a while he raised his head, took out the gun she'd handled at Corey's place, put it in a manila folder, sealed the flap, scrawled across it almost illegibly: "See if you can get anything on this for me. Wanger" with his precinct number.

He picked up the phone. "Send me in a messenger, will you?"

"There's no one around out here right now," the desk sergeant answered.

"Try to find someone, anyone'll do."

The rookie that showed up about ten minutes later was green enough to have fooled a grazing cow.

Wanger remarked, "Where'd they dig you up from?" But he said it well under his breath. After all, everyone has feelings.

"What took you so long?"

"I got in a couple of the wrong rooms. This building's kind of tricky."

Wanger looked at him through blurred eyes. "Take this over and give it in for me. It's a gun. They'll know what to do." Then, with a touch of misgiving, "Will you be able to get there, d'you think?"

The rookie beamed proudly. "Oh, sure, I been sent over there twice already since I been detailed around here."

He turned, came up against the wrong side of the door, where there was no knob, only hinges, looked up and down the seam as though it had played a dirty trick on him. Then he got what the trouble was, shifted over to where the knob was, grabbed it and still couldn't get out right.

"Get your feet out of the way," Wanger coached him with angelic patience. "They're holding it up."

He was too tired even to get sore about it.

"You're still sure of what you told me the other night?" Wanger began, on his second and more detailed questioning of Corey, at headquarters forty-eight hours later.

"Positive. She had the same eyes, mouth, everything, in fact, but the hair, of that girl in black who was at Marjorie Elliott's engagement party the night Bliss met his death two years ago. I could swear it was the same one!"

"Your testimony's doubly welcome to me; it's not only important in itself but it bears out what my own private theory has been in these cases all along: that the woman is one and the same. A theory that, I might add, isn't shared by anyone else."

Corey clenched his fist, bounced it on the tabletop. "If I'd only gotten it sooner, figured out who it was the portrait reminded me of! But I didn't get it in time."

"Undoubtedly you could have saved his life if you'd only made the discovery even an hour earlier that same night. But the breaks fell her way. As it was, you only succeeded in hurrying the thing up, bringing it on all the faster, by insisting you'd seen her somewhere before. She identified you and recognized the danger, realized she had a deadline to work against. And made it—maybe only minutes ahead of your first warning phone call! He died at twenty-one past three in the morning; his wristwatch stopped with the fall."

"And I phoned him at 3:22 or 3:23; I saw the time there in my room!" Corey grimaced anguishedly. "The arrow must have been still vibrating through his heart, he hadn't even toppled to the floor yet!"

"Don't let it get you." The detective tried to brace him up. "It's over now and it's too late. What interests me is that you can be invaluable to me; you're what I've been crying for all along in

this, and now I've got it. At last there's a link between two of
these four men. You didn't know Mitchell, did you?"

"No, I didn't."

"Moran?"

"Him, either."

"But at least you did know two of them, if not the others.
You're the first witness of any sort we've turned up who is in
that position, who overlaps two of these episodes, bridges them.
Don't y'see what you can mean to us?"

Corey looked doubtful. "But I didn't know the two of them
concurrently. I only met Ferguson about eight months ago, at a
cocktail party. Bliss was already dead by that time."

Wanger's face dropped. "So that even through you, any connection between the two of them will have to come by hearsay,
at secondhand."

"I'm afraid so. Even Bliss I only knew the last year or two of
his life. He and Ferguson had sort of drifted apart, got out of
each other's orbit, by then."

"Any trouble between them?" Wanger asked alertly.

"No. Different worlds, that was all. Divergent occupations
and hence divergent interests; brokerage and art. No points of
contact left after they once started to harden into their molds."

"Did either of them mention Mitchell?"

"No, never that I can recall."

"Moran?"

"No."

"Well, Mitchell and Moran are in it somewhere," Wanger
said doggedly. "But we'll let them ride for the present, take
the two we've got. Now, here's what I want you to do for me:
I want you to burrow back in your memory, rake up every par-

ticular mention each of those two made of the other— Bliss of Ferguson and Ferguson of Bliss—and try to recall in just what connection the reference was made, just what subject or topic it had to do with. Women, horses, money, whatever it was. Is that clear? My theory is there is some point at which these four lives cross—maybe other lives, as well. But since I don't know who the others are, I'll have to confine myself to the four I do know of so far. Once I find that point, I may be able to trace the woman *forward*, from there on, since I haven't been able to trace her or her motive *backward*, from the crimes themselves."

Wanger to superior:

"As a matter of fact, to clear the decks I'm going to do what will probably seem to you suicidal, fatal. I'm going to eliminate the woman from my calculations entirely, leave her out of it as completely as though she didn't exist. She only clouds the thing up, anyway. I'm going to concentrate on the four men. Once I can put my finger on the connecting link there is between them, she'll reenter the thing automatically, probably dragging her motive into view."

His superior shook his head dubiously. "It's sort of an inverted technique, to say the least. She commits the murders, so instead of concentrating on her, you concentrate on the victims."

"In self-defense. She'll hold us up forever, like she's already held us up for nearly two solid years. When you can't get in one door, get in another. Even if they don't lead to the same rooms, at least you're in."

"Well, try to get in, even if it's by a chimney," his superior urged plaintively. "The only thing that keeps this from being a big stink is that no one inside or out of the department seems to share your conviction that the four cases have any relation to one another. Presumably to be outwitted by four separate criminals on four different occasions is less of a reflection on us than to be outwitted by the same criminal four times running."

Wanger was coming down the steps at headquarters when he bumped into Corey on his way up them. Corey grabbed him by the arm. "Hold on, you're just the man I want to see."

"What brings you around here at this unearthly hour? I was just on my way home."

"I was playing cards until now, and listen, remember those 'mentions' you asked me to recall if I could—Bliss of Ferguson, and vice versa? Well, one of them popped into my head, so I left the game flat then and there."

"Swell. Come on in and let's hear it," They turned and went up the steps together. Wanger led him into an unoccupied room at the back, snapped on a light. "I get the hell bawled out of me whether I get home late or early," he confessed ruefully, "so half an hour more won't matter."

"Now, I don't know if this is what you want or not, but at least I got something. I wanted to get it to you right away, before I lose it again. Association of ideas brought something back to me. We were playing stud tonight and somebody shoved a stack of chips across the table, said, 'Can't take 'em with you.' That brought Ferguson back to me. We were playing poker down at his studio one night, and I remember him shoving a stack across the table with the same remark. Then that in turn brought back a reference he made at the time to Ken Bliss—and that was what you told me the other day you wanted.

"See how it works? Association of ideas, once removed. He said, 'I haven't had a hand like this since I used to belong to the Friday-Night Fiends.' I said, 'What were the Friday-Night Fiends?' He said, 'Ken Bliss and I and a couple of others were banded together in a sort of informal card-playing club. No dues or charter or anything like that; we'd just meet every other Friday—payday for most of us—for a stud session, each time at a different guy's room. Then we'd all pile into a car we owned shares in, half-soused, and go joyriding through the town, raising cain.'

"That was all he said, just in the space of time it took the dealer to fill up discards around the board. Now is that worth anything to you?"

Wanger whacked him behind the shoulder, so hard that Corey had to grab the table to keep an even balance. "It's the first break I've had!"

Wanger to superior:

"They belonged to a card club together, Bliss and Ferguson. That doesn't sound like much, does it? But it's what I've said I wanted, so I'm not kicking: the point at which their two lives crossed."

"What does that give you?"

"One thread by itself is not much good. Two crossed threads are that much stronger. Cross a few more together at the same place, and you're beginning to get something that'll hold weight. It's the way nets are made.

"Now I've got to do a lot of plodding. I've got to find out the date, that is the year, on which this little amateur social club was banded together. I've got to find out others who were in it, along with Bliss and Ferguson. I've got to find out the dates of the month of the particular Fridays on which they got together.

When I have, I've got to check those dates carefully to see if I can find just what they were up to when, as Ferguson expressed it, they went tearing around half-stewed. It may show up in the blotter of some out-of-the-way police station.

"Then when I've got all that built up, I can start looking for this woman from that point on. I'll have a fulcrum. I won't be suspended in midair the way I am now."

"Outside of all that," commiserated his superior, but strictly off the record, "you've got practically nothing to do. How you going to spend your spare time?"

Ten days later:

"Get anywhere yet?"

"Yeah, like a snail. I've got the year date and I've got the names of the other two members of the Friday-Night Fiends. But there's a blind spot has developed in it that I don't like the looks of. It may make the whole line of investigation worthless if I can't clear it up pretty soon."

"What is it?"

"No Mitchell. He wasn't a member of the card club; his name wasn't among them. I went checking back through dusty police blotters, and I finally hit something, like I figured I might. Four men in a car were pinched on a Friday for drunken and disorderly conduct, reckless driving, smashing a plate-glass window by throwing an empty liquor bottle at it as they went by and finally knocking over a fire hydrant. They spent sixty days apiece in the workhouse, had to pay the damages, and of course their license was taken away from them. Now, three of the names down on the blotter were Bliss, Moran and Ferguson. They gave their right ones, too, thank God. The fourth is a new one, Honeyweather. Also, I got their addresses—at that time—of the blotter. I'll have an easier time now tracing this Honeyweather, the other member, from there on. But if Mitchell had been a member of the card club, he'd have been in the jam along with them, and he's one of the four she's killed. So I'm scared stiff that the card club has nothing to do with the killings and I'm barking up the wrong tree."

"Mitchell may have been ill that particular night, or he'd passed out and been dropped off at his home before they got into all that trouble, or he may have been out of town. I wouldn't give up yet; I'd keep on with it like you are. At least it's a positive line of approach; it's better than nothing at all."

A week later:

"How are you coming now, Wanger?"

"Do you see this look on my face? It's that of a man about to jump off a bridge."

"Fair enough! Only first clean up these Unknown-Woman Murders. Then I'll drive you as far as the bridge approach myself and even pay the toll for you."

"All kidding aside, Chief, it's ghastly. I've finished building the thing up since my last report. I've got it all complete now, not a thing left out. I even filled in the Mitchell blind spot. And now that I'm through—it has no meaning, it doesn't help us at all! It has the same drawback to it that each of these murders in itself has had: there isn't any motive there, from beginning to end, to incite to murder. Nothing they did was criminal enough, injurious enough to anyone, to precipitate a deferred-payment blood feud."

"It may be present but you haven't identified it yet. Let me hear your report anyway."

"I tried to trace this Honeyweather, the fourth member, from the address he gave that night of their quadruple arraignment. And I've lost him entirely. Gone from the face of the earth. I was able to keep up with his movements for about a year afterward—and God knows he moved around plenty! Then he seems to have dropped from sight, vanished as completely as this woman herself has—only without the subsequent reappearances she makes!"

"What line was he in?"

"Seems to have been chronically unemployed. He sat in his room all day pecking away at a typewriter, from what his last landlady tells me. Then he left there and never showed up anywhere else."

"Wait a minute, maybe I can give you a lift on that," his superior said. "Unemployed—pecking away at a typewriter; maybe he was trying to be a writer. They sometimes change their names, don't they? Have you got a pretty recognizable description?"

"Yes, fairly accurate."

"Take it around to the various publishing houses, see if it fits anyone you know. Now, what about Mitchell? You said you cleared that up."

"Yes. He was the bartender of a place they frequented at that time. They took him with them in the car more than once. Chiefly, I gather, because he chiseled liquor from his employer's shelves and brought it along with him each time. So that although he was not a member of the card club itself, he was very much present when they went skylarking around afterward.

Which at least keeps my whole line of investigation from collapsing, the way I was afraid it was going to; those Friday-night tears in the car are still the point at which all their lives intercross. But the main difficulty still remains: they don't seem to have been guilty of anything that would warrant bringing *this* on, what we're up against now."

"Are you sure of that?"

"As far as all police records go, anywhere within the city limits during that period; and I've even covered the nearby outlying communities."

"But don't you realize that it was bound to be something that escaped police attention at the time, otherwise they wouldn't still be at large today? It must have been a crime that was never attributed to them on the official records."

"More than that," Wanger said thoughtfully. "It just occurs to me—it may have been a crime that they didn't even realize they committed themselves. Well, I've got a way of finding *that* out, too! I'm going to sift through the back files of every newspaper that came out, on the particular dates of their get-togethers. It must be in one of them somewhere, hidden, tucked away, not seeming to have anything to do with him. That's what libraries are for. That's where I'll be from now on. The tougher it gets, the harder to lick I get!"

Wanger to Fingerprint Department, by telephone:

"Well, what the hell happened to that gun? D'ja lose it? I'm still waiting for a report."

"What gun? You never sent us any gun, whadaya talking about?" Incoherent squeak, as when a tenor voice goes suddenly falsetto. Then:

"I never *what*? I sent you a gun to be checked over God knows how many weeks ago and not a peep out of you since! I'm still waiting! It wasn't supposed to be a Christmas present, y'know! What kind of a place are you running there, anyway? It's up to you guys to get it back to me, or didn't you know that? You're a fine bunch of crumbs!"

"Listen, thunder voice, we don't needa be told our job by anyone. Who the hell do you think you are, the police commissioner? If y'da sent us a gun to be tested, we'da sent it back to ya! How we gonna get something back to you we never got from you in the first place?"

"Listen, don't get tough with me, whoever you are. I got a gun coming to me and I want it!"

"Aw, look up your assignment and see if that's where you left it!"

Clopp!

City home of a popular and successful writer, three weeks later:

"Mr. Holmes, there's a gentleman in the outside room who insists on seeing you. He won't be put off."

"You know better than to do this! How long have you been working for me?"

"I *told* him you were dictating into the machine, but he says it simply cannot wait. He threatened, if I didn't come in and inform you, to come in himself."

"Where's Sam? Call Sam and have him thrown out! If he gives you any trouble, call the police!"

"But, Mr. Holmes, he *is* the police. That's why I thought I'd better come in and let you——"

"Police be damned! I suppose I parked too long by a fireplug or something! Right while I'm in the middle of the biggest scene in the whole book, too! D'you realize this whole interruption has gone into the machine, that I'll have to start over again from the end of the last record? I'm sorry to do this, Miss Truslow, but you've broken one of my first and most inflexible rules that was impressed on you over and over when you were first taken on to help me with my work. No intrusion while I'm creating, not even if the building is burning down around me! I'm afraid I won't need you anymore after today. You finish up the typing that you have on hand, and Sam will give you your check when you're ready to go home.

"Is this the man? Just what do you mean by forcing yourself in here and creating a disturbance like this? What is it you want to speak to me about?"

Wanger (softly): "Your life."

PART FIVE

HOLMES,
THE LAST ONE

It seemed to me behind my chair there stood a spectre
with a cold and cruel smile, lifeless and motionless.

—DE MAUPASSANT

I

The Woman

THERE WERE FOUR of them in the dormitory room, all in varying stages of night attire. One was sprawled across the bed in reverse, her chin and arms dangling over the foot. One was sitting perched on the windowsill, balanced with one pointed toe touching the floor, like a frozen ballet dancer. The third was sitting on the floor, clasping her reared knees, chin atop them. The fourth and last, the only one audible, was in a chair. Not sitting in it, as that position is commonly understood. She was spread across it flat like a lap robe. One chair arm supported her elbows, her legs rippled across the other. In the middle, where she sank in to meet the part of the chair usually reserved for sitting, a book balanced unsupported, rising and falling with her bodily breath. Rising and falling fairly rapidly at the moment.

"'There's a cabin waiting among the spruce and firs that needs a woman's touch, Miss Judith'," he said.

"'She smiled shyly and her head dropped upon his chest. His strong arms slowly encircled her.'"

At this point the reader's own shoulders twitched ecstatically, as though they were receiving the embrace in question. She let the book slide languishingly to the floor.

"I bet he's just like that himself," she rhapsodized dreamily. "Strong and reliant, and sort of bashful with it. D'you notice how he kept calling her 'Miss Judith' right through to the end, sort of respectful?"

"I bet with you he wouldn't have been that respectful."

The girl on the chair exulted, "You bet not, I would have seen to it he stopped being that formal right after the first chapter."

The one on the bed said, "She's sure got it bad."

"I dreamed about him last night. He rescued me from an igloo that was just going to cave in."

The other three tittered. "What else did he do?"

"That was all there was time for. The eight o'clock bell woke me up—darn it."

"Pass around another cigarette," somebody said.

"There's only one left."

"Oh, what's the difference? We'll get another pack for tomorrow night."

"Yes, and don't forget it's your turn to bring them in next. I supplied this one."

"All right, here goes. We'll have to open the window again. If the smoke gets out in the hall and old Fraser comes along——"

The one in the chair gave a deep sigh that buckled her in the middle momentarily. "Why do you have to be old before you meet anyone thrilling, before anything exciting happens to you?"

"She's still thinking about *him*."

"How do you know he isn't married, and with about thirty-two kids?"

"I know he isn't, he *couldn't* be."

"Why couldn't he?"

"Because it wouldn't be fair.'"

"Poor thing, I hate to see her suffer so."

The one on the bed said impatiently, "Oh, all she does is *talk* about it, and it ends there. If she ever met him face to face she wouldn't know what to do, she'd probably drop through the floor."

The chair sprawler reared defiantly. "Is that so? I'd show you a thing or two. I'd have him eating out of the hollow of my hand in no time."

Her detractor on the bed taunted, "I bet you wouldn't even get past the front door."

"I bet I would, if I ever made up my mind to! How much do you want to bet?"

"How much do *you* want to bet?"

"I'll bet you my whole next month's allowance from home!"

The one on the bed eyed her vindictively. "All right, mine against yours. And you either go through with it or keep still about him from now on. I'm sick of hearing about him."

"Yes, get it out of your system once and for all," one of the more sympathetically inclined listeners suggested. "It's no use just going on pining like this."

The skeptic on the bed said, "How'll we know she's telling the truth when she gets back?"

"I'll bring proof back with me."

"Bring one of his neckties," one of them suggested jocularly.

"No, that's no good, I know something better. She has to bring a snapshot of the two of them standing together."

"And his arm has to be around her," crowed the windowsill sitter. "We want our money's worth!"

"Huh!" snorted the man killer in the chair self-confidently. "That'll be putting it mild; the best parts'll never get on the snapshot. If I ever really go to work on him, he'll probably follow me back here on the end of a leash."

"How'll you get away from here?"

"I've got everything thought out. I've been daydreaming about it for the longest time, in French class and places like that, so I know just what to do. You know how scared stiff Miss Fraser is of epidemics—if you show two red dots on your face she can't get rid of you fast enough. And my people are away right now——"

"You better see that you win," one of the neutrals commiserated, "or you'll be broke for thirty days straight—and don't expect us to lend you any pocket money."

The one bunched on the floor flew apart suddenly. "Fraser!" she hissed warningly. "I hear her step in the hall!"

The room dissolved into a flux of flurried motion, in which they all darted at cross angles to one another. Two of them made for the communicating door to the adjoining room and fled back to their own quarters. The one who had been on the windowsill dove for the recently vacated bed and disappeared with a great welling up of covers.

The one who had been in the chair was left stuck with the cigarette. She snapped out the light and its red ember made hectic spirals around in the dark, in search of a landing place.

"Take this! Take this!" she whispered frenziedly.

"*You* take it!" the unfeeling reply came back. "You were the last one holding it."

It described a parabola out the open window, the bedcovers billowed up a second time, and then there was a sort of heaving silence. An instant later a grimly vigilant head was outlined against the insidiously opened hall door. It sniffed the air suspiciously, remained poised an uncertain moment or two, then finally withdrew, defeated but unconvinced.

When it had inspected the adjoining room, as well, and gone on from there, a whispered conversation in the latter was eagerly resumed.

"Don't you think there's something funny about her? I mean, she's not like the rest of us, she seems older."

"Yes, I've noticed that, too."

"After all, there's nobody here really knows anything about her. Her parents didn't even bring her here when she registered; I heard Miss Fraser say her application was received by mail and she was enrolled on the strength of a recommendation. Who is she? Where did she come from? She suddenly plops down in the middle of us from nowhere and in the middle of the term, too."

"Well, she was transferred."

"Oh, that's what *she* says."

"Nobody's ever seen her people. And she never gets letters from home like the rest of us."

"Why is she so insane about that silly writer? I don't see anything so wonderful about him."

"He has a country place not far from here; maybe that's why she came here—to be near him."

"Maybe she's not a schoolgirl at all."

There was a moment of silent, shivery conjecture. "Then what is she?"

II

Holmes

HOLMES'S ROADSTER WAS crawling along at his usual snail's pace, hugging the extreme outside of the road, German shepherd stiffly erect in the seat beside him, when the taxi flashed by, going the same way he was. He habitually drove in low like that, to help his thinking. He found he could get quite a lot of it done when he was out alone in the car for an airing, just drifting along aimlessly.

He couldn't be positive, of course, but the cab had seemed to him to have just the one girl sitting in the back of it. The reason he figured it that way was the back of her head occupied the exact center of the small oval glass insert in the rear, and when there are two or more passengers they are usually more evenly distributed on the seat than that.

By the time he neared the cutoff that led into his own place, the cab should have been long out of sight, at the clip it had been going, but to his surprise it was still in view ahead as he crested the last rise. It was dawdling along erratically now, as though experiencing a contradiction of orders on its passenger's part.

Just as it came opposite the cutoff, with its warning, T. Holmes, Private Road, No Thoroughfare, stretched across it, three acoustically perfect screams winged up from it. The next moment, the door flung outward and the figure of a girl either jumped or was flung bodily onto the soft turf edging the road. She rolled over once in a complete somersault, then came to a stop right side up. The taxi put on speed and spurted down the road, red tail glowering vindictively.

Holmes glided to a stop opposite her a moment later and got out. She was in a sideways sitting position now, clutching her instep with both hands. The German shepherd undutifully remained in the car, as though that was his first love, rather than his master.

"Hurt yourself?" Holmes bent over her, took her below the arms and helped her to her feet. She immediately teetered against him.

"I can't stand up on one of them. What'll I do?"

"Better come into my place a minute. It's right down the way there."

He helped her into the car, drove the short distance down the private road, helped her out again in front of a typical remodeled-for-city-occupancy farmhouse. The dog didn't have sense enough to follow even then, until Holmes had turned and growled at it, "Come on in, you fool. What do you want to do, stay out all night?" The dog leaped over the side of the car and approached the door independently, with an air of not belonging to anyone.

A manservant opened to the clomp of the Colonial knocker affixed to the door. He greeted Holmes with the familiarity bred of long years of association. "Well, did you get a bang-up finish for that chapter troubling your mind?"

"I did have one," said Holmes somewhat moodily, "but it was knocked right out of my head again. This young lady's had a mishap. Help me get her to a chair, then go out and put the car in."

The two of them helped her down a long pine-paneled living room that ran the entire depth of the house, with a gigantic conical fireplace of cobbled stones set into one side, from floor to ceiling. That is, the trim was ceiling high, the aperture itself was about shoulder height or a little less.

She attempted to stop and sink down when she had reached a large overstuffed chair standing out before it, with its back to the salmon-pink glow. The manservant quickly gave her a little hitch onward, toward another a few paces away. "Not that one—that's his inspiration chair."

Seated, Holmes studied her by the firelight, aided by the watery glow of light from the ceiling. The electricity was obviously generated on the premises, judging by its insufficiency.

She was young, and the mere fact that everything about her tried to convey the exact opposite impression showed how young she really was. Eighteen; nineteen at the very outside. Her hair had probably been golden when she was a child, it was darkening to chestnut now, but with golden overtones still lingering in it. Her eyes were blue.

She had acquired, if nothing else, a generous coating of leaves and twigs in her roll by the roadside just now. She brushed at them sketchily, almost as though she hated to efface them until she was sure he had taken note of what bad shape she was in.

"What happened?" he said as soon as Sam had left to see about the car.

"The usual thing. Whenever you see a girl come out of

a car without waiting for it to stop, you can draw your own conclusions."

"But it was a city cab, wasn't it?" It occurred to him it was a little far out for that sort of thing.

"And the ideas in it were city ideas." She didn't seem to want to talk about it any further.

"I guess we'd better have a doctor in to look at that foot of yours."

She didn't show any particular eagerness at the suggestion. "Maybe it'll go down if I just stay off it."

"It hasn't gone up any, from what I can see," he pointed out.

She withdrew it a little behind the first one, so that its outline wasn't so distinct.

Sam had come back. "Sam, who's the nearest doctor to us?"

"Doc Johnson, I reckon. He don't know us. I can try him if you want."

"It's pretty late—maybe he won't want to come," she mentioned.

Sam returned to report, "He'll be here in half an hour."

She said, "Oh," sort of flatly.

After a while, while they were waiting, she said, "I've always wondered what you were like."

"Oh, then you know who I am?"

"Who doesn't? I've read you from *A* to *Z*." She sighed soulfully. "Imagine sitting here in the same room with you!"

He turned away. "Cut that stuff out."

"And at least you're like you should be," she went on, undeterred. "I mean so many of these people that write red-blooded outdoor stuff are skinny anemic little runts wrapped in blankets. You at least cut a figure that a girl can get her teeth into."

"You oughta be poured over waffles," he let her know disgustedly.

Her eyes roamed the raftered ceiling, flickering with flame reflections like sea waves. "You live in this big place all alone?"

"I come out here to work." If there was a gentle hint in that, it glanced off her.

"What a fireplace; I bet you could stand up on the inside of it."

"They used to smoke whole hams and turkeys inside it in the old days; the hooks are still set into the inside of the chimney. It's almost too big, takes it too long to draw and get heat up. I tried to cut it down by refining it, putting in a dummy top and sides of zinc."

"Oh, yes, I see that chink that seems to border it all around; I thought it was a fault in the stones."

Sam was thrusting at the fire with a heavy iron poker when the doctor's knock sounded at the door. He stood it up against the stone facing, went out to admit him. Holmes followed him into the hall to greet the doctor. He thought he heard her give a sobbing little moan of excruciation behind him, but the doctor's noisy ingress drowned it out.

When they came in a moment later, her face was contorted and all the color seemed to have left it. The iron poker lay horizontal on the floor, as though it had toppled down of its own weight.

"Let's have a look," the doctor said. He felt gently with his fingers, and she winced, gave an inarticulate little cry. The doctor clicked his tongue. "You've got a bad contusion there, I should say so! But it's not a sprain, more like one of the little cartilages is smashed, from something heavy dropping on it.

Wrap it up in cotton wool. You'll have to spare that foot for a day or two, give it a chance to mend."

Even while the overflow wrung from her by pain slowly trickled out of the corner of each eye, the look she gave Holmes seemed to hold something of triumph in it.

Afterward, when the doctor had gone, he said, "I don't know how we're going to do it. The station's a forty-minute pull from here, and I don't even know if there are any more trains in to-night. I could drive you all the way in to the city myself, but we'd get there about daylight."

"Can't I stay?" she said wistfully. "I won't bother you."

"It isn't that. I'm single and I'm alone in the house. Even Sam sleeps out over the garage."

"Och." She tossed that off like a puffball. "The dog'll be chaperon enough."

"Well, er, won't your people worry about you if you stay away overnight?"

Something like a choked laugh sounded in her throat. "Oh, sure, three days from now. They're in New Mexico. By the time they hear I wasn't home, I'll be home all over again."

He gave Sam a look and Sam gave him one. "Fix up that ground-floor room that has the cot in it for the lady, Sam," he said finally.

"Freddy Cameron's the name," the childish-looking figure ensconced in the chair supplied. "Short for Frederica, you know."

They sat there in silence, waiting for Sam to get the room ready. Holmes sat staring down at the floor, she sat staring at him with all the unconcealed candor of a child.

"Why do you keep all those rifles and shotguns stacked up in the corner?"

"Because I do a lot of hunting when I'm not working."

"Are they loaded?"

"Sure they're loaded." He waited a moment and then he added, "They give a terrible kickback when they're fired."

"G'night, Mr. Holmes and lady," Sam called on his way out. The front door closed after him.

The silence became almost cottony, the sort of thing that can be tasted in the mouth.

"Why don't we say something?" she suggested after about a quarter of an hour.

His eyes flicked over her, then down to the floor again, for answer.

There was something wary about the slight deflection.

She bunched her shoulders defensively, looked behind her. "Something about this place, it gets you. It's like—something was going to happen."

"It's like," he concurred curtly, and got up and left her without anything further. He moved up the stairs to the upper floor with almost painful deliberation, head bowed as though he were listening intently.

A cooling log ash exploded in the fireplace; his shoulders squared off, then relaxed again. Then the heavy, oily stillness came rolling back again and obliterated the momentary sound. His door closed, up above somewhere.

Sam came in and found them sitting at the table together.

"What's this?" he cried with mock outrage that had an undercurrent of pique to it.

"The Number-Two Boy rustled it up for him this morning. But she has no luck, he won't eat."

"He's thinking of a plot," Sam suggested.

Holmes gave him a startled look, as though the remark was disconcertingly shrewd. He filled a saucer from his cup, put it on the floor. The German shepherd came over and noisily siphoned it up.

"Well, is the plot finished yet?" she wanted to know presently.

"Incomplete," Holmes said. He had been watching the dog. "But I'll get it later." He took up his cup, drained it, held it out to her for more.

He got up, threw her a brief, "See you tonight," and went into the living room.

"What does he mean, 'See you tonight'?" she asked Sam blankly. "What am I supposed to be, invisible until then?"

"He's going to produce now." Sam went in after him, as though his presence was required to set things in order. She watched from the doorway. Sam shifted the "inspiration chair," cocked his head at it, readjusted the chair with hairline precision.

"Does that have to be in the exact same place each time?" she asked incredulously. "I suppose if it was two inches out of line he couldn't think straight."

"Shh!" Sam silenced her imperiously. "If it ain't even with that diagonal pattern of the carpet, it distracts him."

Holmes was standing looking out the window, already lost to the world. He made an abrupt backhand gesture of dismissal. "Get out! Here it comes now."

Sam tiptoed out with almost ludicrous haste, frenziedly motioning her before him. She stood there a moment outside the closed door, unabashedly eavesdropping. Holmes's voice filtered through in a droning singsong, talking into the dictating machine: "Chinook mushed on through the snow wastes, face a mask of vengeance under his fur parka——"

Sam wouldn't leave her in peace even there. "Don't stand this close, you're liable to make the floor creak."

She turned away reluctantly, limping on her one slippered foot. "So that's how it's done. And there must never be the slightest variation in detail, not even in the way his chair stands."

Sam poised himself, watch in hand, outside the door, one fist upraised in striking position. He waited until the sixtieth second had ticked off, then brought his fist down. "Five o'clock!" he called warningly.

Holmes came out haggard, hair awry, shirt open down to his abdomen, cuffs open, shoelaces untied, even his belt buckle unfastened.

A prim, mousy little figure of a middle-aged woman, sitting under the antlered hat rack near the door, stood up. She wore an ill-fitting tweed suit, steel-rimmed spectacles, and had her graying hair drawn tightly back into an unsightly little knot at the nape of her neck.

"I'm the new typist, Mr. Holmes. Mr. Trent says he hopes I'll be more satisfactory than the last one he sent you."

The Cameron girl had come to the doorway of her room, opposite them, drawn by the sound of his emergence.

"I'm afraid the damage has been done already," he said with a glance at her. "Did you come prepared to stay?"

"Yes." She indicated a venerable Gladstone bag on the floor beside her. "Mr. Trent explained the work would have to be done on the premises."

"Well, I'm glad you got here. I've already done six chapters into the machine. I don't know how fast you are, but it'll take you at least three or four days to catch up."

"I'm more accurate and painstaking than I am speedy," she

let him know primly. "I pride myself on never having had so much as a comma misplaced on any of my typescripts." She folded her hands limply together, dangled them out before her.

"Sam, carry Miss—I didn't get your name."

"Miss Kitchener."

"Carry Miss Kitchener's bag up to the front second-floor room."

The Cameron girl came toward him, a look of sulky disapproval on her face, as soon as he was alone. "So we're going to have Lydia Pinkham with us for a while."

"You seem put out."

"I am." She wasn't being playful about it, either; she was seething. "A woman likes the run of the place. This was ideal."

He gave her a long, level look. "I'll bet it was," he said dryly, turning away at last.

Sam said later, "We're sure getting a run of women out here! Maybe you better do your work in town, where it's nice and lonely, after this, Mr. Holmes."

"I have an idea they'll be thinning out soon." Holmes answered, brushing his hair at the mirror.

The three of them sat back after Sam had taken out the dessert plates. Freddy Cameron still had the sulky look on her face. Throughout the meal she had tried, much to his amusement, to give the other woman the impression she was a legitimate member of the household.

"Sam," he called. And when the man had returned to the doorway, "How long since you've had a night off?"

"Pretty long. But ain't no use in having one out here. There's no place to go."

"Tell you what I'll do. I'll treat you to one in the city. I'll drive you over to the station when I go out for my usual evening spin. There are some things I want you to stop in and get at the flat in town while you're there, anyway."

"I'd sure like that! But will you be able to get along without me, Mr. Holmes?"

"Why not? You'll be back by midmorning. Miss Cameron can rustle up breakfast for me, like she did today."

Her face brightened for almost the first time since the typist's arrival. "Can I?"

"And I can build my own fire when I'm ready to start work in the morning. Just see that there's enough wood on hand."

It was nearly eleven when he drove slowly back to the house alone, after dropping off his loyal retainer at the depot. The German shepherd, aloof as usual, sat in the seat beside him. The countryside was as still as a grave. The road was empty; no speeding city taxi passed him tonight.

He put the car away himself, opened the house door with his own key. It seemed strange; he was so used to having Sam do these little things for him.

The Cameron girl was standing out at the foot of the stairs, listening. A sound like frightened, low-pitched sobbing reached him from above.

She smiled inscrutably, thumbed the staircase. "The old maid's walking out on you."

"What d'you mean?"

"She's packing up to go. She's got the heebie-jeebies. Somebody threw a rock through her window warning her to clear out."

"Why didn't you go up and calm her at least?" he snapped.

"I didn't have to. She came tearing down here to me in an 1892 flannel nightie and practically jumped into my lap for protection. That's only the trailer you're listening to now.

I looked up the trains for her, as long as she wanted to leave that bad."

"It would have surprised me very much if you hadn't."

She ignored that. "Some mischievous kids must have done it, don't you think?"

"Undoubtedly," he said as he started up. "Only there don't happen to be any for miles around here."

Miss Kitchener was packing things into the Gladstone bag, between whiffs at a bottle of smelling salts. There was a fist-size rock on the table, and a crudely penciled scrap of paper that had been wrapped around it lay nearby. He read the message on it.

Get out of that house before morning
or you won't live to regret it.

One of the small partition panes in the window was shattered into a star-shaped remnant.

"You're not going to let a little thing like that get you, are you?" he suggested.

"Oh, I couldn't sleep a wink tonight after this!" she snuffled. "I'm nervous enough other nights as it is, even in the city."

"It's just a practical joke."

She paused uncertainly in her packing. "Wh-who do you suppose . . . ?"

"I couldn't say," he said decisively, as though to discourage further questioning on that score. "Did you look out, try to see who was down there at the time?"

"Dear me, no! I ran for my life down the stairs as soon as I'd finished reading it. I—I feel so much better now that you're back, Mr. Holmes. There's something about having a man in the house——"

"Well," he said. "I don't want to oblige you to stay here if you're going to be frightened and uncomfortable. I'm willing to drive you in to the station and you still have plenty of time to make the quarter-of-twelve train. You can do the typing next week in the city, when I come back. It's entirely up to you."

The avenue of escape he was offering obviously appealed to her. He saw her look almost longingly toward her open bag. Then she took a deep breath, gripped the foot rail of the bed with both hands as if to steel herself. "No," she said. "I was sent out here to do this work for you, and I've never yet failed to carry out anything that was expected of me. I shall stay until the work is complete!" But she spoiled the fine courage of the sentiments she was expressing by stealing a surreptitious after glance at the shattered window.

"I think you'll be all right," he said quietly, with a half-formed little smile at the corner of his mouth. "The dog's an effective guarantee that no one will get in the house from outside. And my own room's right down at the other end of the hall." He turned to go, then turned back to her again from the doorway. "There's a small revolver kicking around in one of my bureau drawers somewhere; would you feel any better if I looked for it and let you keep it here with you tonight?"

She gave a squeak of repulsion, palmed her hands at him hastily. "No, no, that would frighten me more than the other thing! I can't bear the sight of firearms of any description, I'm deathly afraid of them!"

"All right, Miss Kitchener," he said soothingly. "You're showing a considerable amount of gallantry in remaining—even though there's really nothing to be worried about—and I won't forget to speak favorably to Mr. Trent about it."

The Cameron girl was in the far corner of the living room,

turning over a rifle in her hands, when he appeared unexpectedly in the doorway a few moments later. His descent must have
been quieter than he realized.

He clasped hands behind his back, tilting the tail of his coat
up out of the way. "I wouldn't monkey around with any of those
if I were you. I think I already told you last night they're kept
loaded."

She looked over at him, hesitated a moment before putting it
down, even turned full face toward him with it still clasped in
her hands but crosswise to her own body.

He didn't move. There was a dancing quality in his eyes, as
though his muscular coordination was prepared to meet a need
for instantaneous action, but he didn't show it in any other way.

She stood the gun up against the wall, ostentatiously brushed
her hands. "Sorry. Everything I seem to do is wrong."

His hands unclasped, the skirt of his coat fell flat. "Oh, no, I
wouldn't say that. Everything you seem to do is right."

He sat down in the "inspiration chair." She hovered around
uncertainly in the background. "Am I intruding?"

"You mean at the moment or by and large?"

"I mean at the moment. By and large I am, I don't need to be
told that."

"No, you're not intruding at the moment. I don't mind your
being in here."

"Where you can keep an eye on me," she finished for him
with a satiric laugh. Her eyes went up toward the raftered ceiling. "Did she decide to stay?"

"Much to your regret."

She sighed elaborately. "We either understand each other too
well or not at all."

That was the last thing either of them said. The fire had

dwindled to a garnet glow, dark as port. The rest of the room was all blue shadow. Just their two faces stood out, pale ovals against the surrounding gloom. A cricket chirped in the velvety silence outside that pressed down, smothered the house like a feather bolster.

He rose to his feet at last, and all you could see rising was the oval of his face; the rest of him already blended into the shadows. He went outside to the stairs, and the scuffing measure of his tread was audible going slowly up them. She stayed on in there, with the garnet embers and the guns.

He closed the door of his room after him, but he didn't put on the light. It was hard to make him out in the India-ink blackness. White suddenly peered faintly over there by the door, in two long columns and a little triangular wedge, and he'd doffed his coat without moving away from before the door seam. A chair shifted, and the white manifestations ebbed lower on it but still there up against the door. A shoe dropped an inch or two, with the sound a shoe makes; then its mate.

The cricket went on outside, and the silence went on inside, and the night went on outside and in. Once, an hour before dawn, a faint disembodied stirring of air seemed to come into the room, but not from the direction of the window, from the direction of the door—as though he had eased it narrowly open without permitting the latch to make any sound. A floorboard creaked in the distance, somewhere far below. Maybe it was just the wood contracting from the increasing night-long coldness. Or maybe stealthy pressure had been put upon it.

Nothing else sounded after that. After a long while, the extra little swirl of air was cut off again. Outside, an owl hooted in a tree and the stars began to pale.

The Cameron girl was unusually vivacious at breakfast, perhaps because she had had the making of it. She was whistling blithely when Holmes came down, a derelict with a shadowy jawline and soot under his eyes. Miss Kitchener was there ahead of him, shining with soap and water, her nocturnal timidity a thing of the past—at least until the coming night.

"You ladies'll have to excuse me," he said, tracing a hand down his sandpapery face as he sat down.

"It's your house, after all," Freddy Cameron pointed out.

Miss Kitchener contented herself with a thin lipped smile, as though there were no excuse for personal untidiness under any circumstances.

The German shepherd came muzzling up to him, evidently remembering yesterday. He ignored it. Freddy Cameron breathed, so low he barely caught it, "No poison test today?"

He shoved his chair back. "Sam'll be back about noon, to take up where he left off. I'm going in there now and expect to be left undisturbed."

"I'll go upstairs and begin my typing," Miss Kitchener said. "I don't believe you'll hear me from where you are."

"I'll paint Easter eggs," Freddy Cameron said disgruntledly

He closed the living-room door after him, thrust cords of wood into the fireplace, kindled a wedge of newspaper under them. He stripped the oilcloth hood off the dictating machine that stood on the table, adjusted it to the best of his ability but with an air of somewhat baffled uncertainty, as though Sam had usually been delegated to attend to this detail along with all the others. The "inspiration chair," he noticed, was slightly out of true with the diagonal pattern of the carpet. He shifted it slightly, smiling a little to himself, as if at his own idiosyncrasies. Then he picked up the speaking tube appended to the machine, sat back, everything in readiness for a long day's creative work. Everything but one thing. . . .

The apparatus made a muted whirr, waiting. The necessary flow of thought wouldn't seem to come. Inspiration appeared to be log-jammed. He glanced helplessly up at the row of his own books on a shelf, as if wondering how he'd done it before.

A floorboard creaked unexpectedly somewhere near at hand. He whirled around in the chair, frowning menacingly at the supposed interruption.

There was no one in the room with him at all; the door was still securely closed. The flames leaped higher behind him, filling the cavern of the fireplace with heat and a crimson rose glow.

The Cameron girl snapped her head around, found his eyes boring into her from the doorway some five minutes later. "Wh-what happened?" she faltered uneasily. "No quarantine this morning?"

"I seem to have hit an air pocket. Come in here, will you? I want to talk to you. Maybe that'll help to get me started."

"You sure you want me in there in the holy of holies?" she wanted to know almost frightenedly.

"I'm sure," he said in a flinty voice.

She made her way in ahead of him, looking back across her shoulder at him the whole way. He closed the door on the two of them. "Sit down."

"*That* chair? I thought no one else was allowed——"

"That's Sam's line of talk." His eyes fixed themselves on her piercingly. "What's the difference between one chair and another?" The question almost seemed to have a special meaning.

She sank into it without further protest. He squatted down,

adding an extra log or two to the fire, which was only now beginning to draw, as though he'd had to start it a second time. Then he sat back diagonally opposite her, in a chair she had occupied whenever she had been in here before. He seemed to be watching her closely, as though he'd never seen her before.

"What'll I talk about?" she suggested presently.

He didn't answer, just kept watching her. A minute or two ticked by; the only sound in the room with them was the steadily increasing hum from the fireplace.

"Deep thought," she said mockingly.

"Let me feel your hand a minute," he said unexpectedly. She extended it to him indolently. The palm was perfectly dry. The wrist was steady.

He flung it back at her with such unexpected force that it struck her across the chest. He was on his feet. "Come on, get out of that chair fast," he said hoarsely. "You sure had me fooled. What's your racket, kid?"

But before she had a chance to answer, he was already over at the door, had thrown it open, was thumbing her out past him with an urgency that had something tingling about it.

"What's the matter with you, anyway?" she drawled reproachfully as she regained her own doorway opposite.

"Keep out of the way for a while; don't come in here, no matter what you hear. Got that straight?" Some of the rough edge left his voice as he called up the stairs with suddenly regained urbanity, "Miss Kitchener, could I speak to you down here a minute?"

The diligent pitter-patter of her typing, which had been like soft rain on a roof, broke off short and she came down unhesitatingly, at her usual precise, fussy little gait.

He motioned her in. "How far have you gotten?" he asked, closing the door.

"I'm midway through the opening chapter," she announced, beaming with complacency.

"Sit down. The reason I called you is I'm changing this lead character's name to— No, sit down there, right where you are."

"That's your chair, isn't it?"

"Oh, any chair. Sit down while I discuss this with you." He forced her to take it by preempting the other one.

She lowered a spine stiff as a ramrod to the outermost edge of it, contacting it by no more than half an inch.

"Will changing his name give you any extra work? Has he appeared by name yet in the part you've already transcribed?"

She was up again with alacrity. "Just a moment, I'll go up and make sure——"

He motioned her down again. "No, don't bother." And then with mild wonderment. "You were just going over that part, how is it you can't recall offhand? Well, anyway, it occurred to me that in Northern stories readers are used to identifying French-Canadian characters with the villain, and therefore it might be advisable to—Miss Kitchener, are you listening to me? What's the matter, are you ill?"

"It's too warm in this chair, the heat of the fire. I can't stand it."

Without warning he reached forward, seized one of her hands before she could draw it back. "You must be mistaken. How can you say the chair's too warm for you? Your hand's ice-cold—trembling with cold!" He frowned. "At least let me finish what I have to say to you."

Her breathing had become harshly audible, as though she had asthma. "No, no!"

They both gained their feet simultaneously. He pressed her down by the shoulder, firmly but not roughly, so that she sank into the chair again. She attempted to writhe out of it sideways this time. Again he gripped her, pinned her down. Her spectacles fell off.

"Why is your face so white? Why are you so deathly afraid?"

She seemed to be in the throes of hysteria, beyond reasoning. A knife unexpectedly flashed out from somewhere about her—her sleeve, perhaps—and was upraised against him across the back of the chair. Her hand was quick; his hand was quicker. He throttled it by the wrist, pinning it down over the chair top; it turned a little, and the knife fell out, glanced off the low fire screen behind her and into the flames.

"That's a funny implement for a typist to be carrying around with her; do you use that in your work?"

She was struggling almost maniacally against him now; something seemed to be driving her to a frenzy. He was exerting his strength passively, holding her a prisoner in the chair with one hand riveted at the base of her throat. He was standing offside to her, however, not directly before her. She alone was in a straight line with the fireplace.

"Let me up—let me up!"

"Not until you speak," he grunted.

She crumpled suddenly, seemed to collapse inwardly, was suddenly a limp bundle there in the chair. "There's a gun in there, above the zinc partition—trained on this chair! Any minute the heat will— A sawed-off shotgun filled with——"

"Who put it there?" he probed relentlessly.

"I did! Quick, let me up!"

"Why? Answer me, why?"

"Because I'm Nick Killeen's widow—and I came here to kill you, Holmes!"

"That's all," he said briefly, and stepped back.

He took his hand away too late. As it broke contact, there was a blinding flash behind her that lit up his face, a roar, and a dense puff of smoke swirled out around her, as though blown out of the fireplace by a bellows worked in reverse.

She heaved convulsively one more time, as though still attempting to escape by reflex alone, then deflated again, staring at him through the smoke haze that veiled her.

"You're all right," he assured her quietly. "I emptied it out before I started the fire up a second time, only left the powder charge in it. The dictation machine saved me; you must have accidentally brushed against the lever, turned it on, when you came in here last night. It recorded the whole proceeding, from the first warning creak of the floor to the replacing of the zinc sheet that roofs the fireplace. Only I couldn't tell which one of you it was; that's why I had to give you the chair test."

The door flashed open and the Cameron girl's frightened white face peered in at them. "What was that?"

He was, strangely enough, twice as rough spoken and curt to her as he had been to the woman in the chair, the way one is to a puppy or a child that can't be held responsible for its actions. "Stay out of here," he bellowed, "you damned nuisance of an autograph-hunting, hero-worshiping school brat, or I'll come out there, turn you over my knee and give you a spanking that'll make you need cotton wool someplace else besides your ankle!"

The door closed again twice as quickly as it had opened, with a gasp of shocked incredulity.

He turned back to the limp, deflated figure still cowering there in the chair. She seemed to hang suspended in a void; she had lost one personality without regaining another. His voice dropped again to ordinary conversational pitch, as with an adult. "What were you going to do to *her*— in case it had worked?" he asked curiously.

She was still suffering from shock, but she managed a weak smile. "Exactly nothing at all. She wasn't even on my list. She couldn't have endangered me. I might have tied her up in order to get away, that's all."

"At least you're fair-minded in your death dealing," he conceded grudgingly. He watched her for a moment, then went over and poured her a drink without turning his back on her. "Here. You seem to be all in shreds. Knit yourself up again."

She tottered waveringly erect at last, one hand out to the chair back. Then little by little a change came over her. She seemed to fill out before his eyes, gain color, body, like those outline drawings they had once given to a child named Cookie Moran. The life-force, that inextinguishable thing, flowed back into her. Not the cold, spinsterish tide that had been Miss Kitchener; something warmer, brighter. Though her hair was still artfully streaked with gray and drawn tightly back, the last vestiges of the prissy Miss Kitchener seemed to peel away, roll off her like a transparent cellophane wrapping. She was somehow a young, more vibrant woman. A woman who knew no fear, a woman who knew how to admit defeat gracefully. But a vengeful sort of grace it was, even now.

"Well, I got them all but you, Holmes. Nick will overlook that. I'm only a woman, after all. Go ahead, call the police, I'm ready."

"I am the police. Holmes was hijacked into safety weeks ago; he's lying low in Bermuda. I've been living his life for him ever since, tearing the covers off his old books and reading them over again into the machine, waiting for you to show up. I was afraid the dog would give me away; it showed so plainly I wasn't its master."

"I should have noticed that," she admitted. "Overconfidence must have made me careless. Everything went like clockwork with all the others—Bliss and Mitchell and Moran and Ferguson."

"Look out," he warned her dryly, "I'm getting it all on there." He thumbed the dictation machine, making its faint whirring sound again.

"Do you take me for the usual petty-larceny criminal for gain, trying to cover up what he's done, trying to welsh out of it?" There was unutterable contempt in the look she gave him. "You have a lot to learn about me! I glory in it! I want to shout it from the housetops, I want the world to know!" She took a quick step over beside the recording apparatus; her voice rose triumphantly into the speaking tube. "I pushed Bliss to his death! I gave cyanide to Mitchell! I smothered Moran alive in a closet! I shot Ferguson through the heart with an arrow! This is Julie Killeen speaking. Do you hear me, Nick, do you hear me? Your debt is paid—all but one.

There, Detective, there's your case. Now bring on *your* revenge. To me it's a citation!"

"Sit down a minute," he said. "There's no hurry. It's taken me two and a half years to catch up with you; a few minutes more won't matter. I want to talk to you."

And when she had sat down, he said, "So you helpfully put it all on the record for me. All but one thing. You neglected to add why; what this outstanding debt was. I happen to know—now, I didn't for years. It was what held me up. I found out just in the nick of time—for Holmes's sake, anyway. If I hadn't he—the real Holmes—would have been where the rest are by now."

"*You* happen to know why!" Sparks seemed to dart from her eyes. "You couldn't, no, nor anyone else. Did you live through it? Did you see it with your own eyes? A dry line or two on some forgotten, dust-covered police report! But it still stings in my heart.

"It's a long time ago now, as time goes, and yet all I have to do is shut my eyes and he's beside me again, Nick, my husband. And the pain wells up around me again, the hate, the rage, the sick, cold loss. All I have to do is shut my eyes and it's yesterday again, that long-past unforgotten yesterday."

III

Flashback: The Little Casket Around the Corner

"For better or for worse, in sickness or in health, until death do ye part?"

"I do."

"I now pronounce you man and wife. Whom God hath joined together, let no man put asunder. You may kiss the bride."

They turned toward each other shyly. She drew the filmy veil clear of her face. Her eyes drooped closed as his lips met hers in the sacramental kiss. She was Mrs. Nick Killeen now, not Julie Bennett anymore.

The members of their wedding party came crowding around; they were engulfed in a surging surf of bobbing heads, back-slapping hands, congratulatory voices. The bridesmaids' tinted chiffon hats swept over her face one by one like colored gelatin slides, dyeing it without obscuring it, while each gave her a little peck of benediction. Through all the commotion, his eyes and hers kept seeking each other, as if to say, "*You're* all that really matters to me, you, over there."

Then they were side by side again, Mr. and Mrs. Nick

Killeen, her hand tucked submissively under his arm, as a wife's should be, her step matched to his, her heart beating his music. Down the long, vaulted church aisle they moved, toward where the doors stood open wide and the future, their future, waited. And behind them, two by two, came the bridesmaids like a bed of mobile flowers, yellow, azure, lilac, pink.

The apsed doorway receded overhead, gave way to a night sky soft as velvet, pricked with a single star, the evening star. Promising things, long life and happiness and laughter; promising things—but with a wink.

Their attendants hung back, as if bonded in some mischievous conspiracy, as the two principals unsuspectingly started down the short, spreading flight of church steps. The foremost of a short line of cars that had been held in readiness a few doors up the street meshed gears and started slowly forward to receive them. A gust of surreptitious giggling swept over those crowded in the doorway behind them. Hands sought paper bags, and the first few swirls of rice began to mist the steps. The bride threw up her arm to ward off the bombardment, huddled closer to the groom. Squeals of glee were emitted, the air whitened with the falling grains.

There was a sudden caterwauling of hysterical brakes; a large black shape, blurred for a moment by its very unexpectedness, careened around the corner of the church. It skimmed over the curb, nearly threatened to mount the steps themselves for a moment. Then by some miracle of maniac steering it veered off, straightened out, revealed itself for a split second as a black sedan, then shot forward into blurred velocity again. A series of ear-splitting detonations had punctuated the whole incredible apparition, and reflected flashes traced it from windowpane to windowpane along the lower floors of the row houses opposite.

In its wake a noxious cloud of black smoke blanketed the church steps and those on them, as though an evil spirit had passed that way, and only began to thin out long after the malignant red taillight had twisted from sight at the far upper end of the street.

The laughter and playful shouts had changed to strangled coughs and splutterings. Then there was a sudden silence, as of premonition. In it, a voice spoke a name. The bride spoke her husband's name. "Nick!" Just once, in a hushed, terrified voice. An instant longer they stood down there motionless at the bottom of the steps, side by side, just as they had left the church. Then all at once she stood alone, and he lay at her feet.

The others broke, came milling down off the steps, fluttering around her. In the middle of them all his face peered up at her, like a white pebble lying at the bottom of a deep pool. There was a tiny fleck of red, a comma, so to speak, down near the bottom of her snowy veil. She kept staring at it as if hypnotized. His face didn't move. Not a comma, no; a period.

Minutes went by that had no meaning anymore. She was a statue in white, the one motionless, the one fixed thing, in all the eddying and swirling about. Voices shouting suggestions reached her as from another world, holding no meaning. "Open his shirt! Get these girls out of here, put them in the cars and send them home!"

Hands were extended toward her, trying to lead her away. "My place is here," she murmured tonelessly.

"Stunned," someone said. "Don't let her stand there like that; see if you can get her to go with you."

She motioned briefly, mechanically, and they let her be.

In the welter of sounds a dismal, clanging bell approached in the distance, rushing through the streets. Then it stopped short.

A black bag stood open at her feet. "Gone," a low voice said. A girl screamed somewhere close at hand. It wasn't she.

The black bag was held partly toward her. "Here, let me give you——"

She motioned them aside with one hand, the one with the new gold wedding band on it. "Just let me hold my husband in my arms a moment. Just let me say goodbye." She knelt over him, with a great welling up of white tulle around her like a snowdrift stirred by the wind. The two heads joined, as they had been meant to join, but only one gave the caress. Those hovering closest heard a soft whisper. "I won't forget."

Then she was erect again, the straightest one among all of them; like ice, like white fire. A whimpering bridesmaid plucked helplessly at her sleeve. "Please come away now, *please*, Julie."

She didn't seem to hear. "How many were in that car, Andrea?"

"I saw five, I think."

"That is what I saw, too, and I have such very good eyes. What was the license number of that car, Andrea?"

"I don't know, I didn't have time——"

"I did. D3827. And I have such a very good memory."

"Julie, don't, you're frightening me. Why aren't you crying?"

"I am, where you can't see it. Come with me, Andrea. I'm going back inside the church."

"To pray?"

"No, to make a vow. Another vow to Nick."

IV

Postmortem on Nick Killeen

"So THAT WAS it, and you've repaid your debt," Wanger said musingly, "and nothing we can do to you now can take away the satisfaction of your accomplishment, is that it? No punishment that you receive from us can touch you—inside, where it really matters, is that right?"

She didn't answer.

"Yes, I had you figured that way all along, and now I see that I had you figured right. Sure, imprisonment won't be any punishment to you, no, nor even the chair itself, if they should happen to give you that. There isn't a flicker of remorse in your eyes, there isn't a shadow of fear in your heart."

"There isn't. You read me right."

"The state can't punish you, can it? But I can. Listen, Julie Killeen. "You haven't avenged Nick Killeen. You only think you have, but you haven't. On the night that Bliss, Mitchell, Ferguson, Holmes and Moran tore past those church steps, howling drunk in their car, a man crouched at the first-floor window of a rooming house opposite, watching for the two of you, a gun in his hand, waiting for you to come out. He'd missed Killeen going in for some reason; maybe the cab Killeen arrived in formed an impediment in his line of fire, maybe there were too many people around him, maybe he reached his death post too late. And so he stayed there; he wasn't going to miss him coming out.

"He didn't.

"He raised his gun as you and your husband came down the steps. He sighted at Nick, and he pulled the trigger. The car streaked by in between at that instant, with its exhaust tube exploding a mile a minute. But his bullet found its mark, over the car's low top. It was a freak of timing that wouldn't have happened again in a hundred years, that couldn't have happened if he had tried to arrange it that way. The very reflections of the backfiring along the row of unlighted windowpanes helped to cover up his flash.

"There's your punishment, Julie Killeen. You've sent four innocent men to their deaths, who had nothing to do with killing your husband."

He hadn't reached her with that, he could tell; there was still the same glaze of icy imperviousness all over her. There was disbelief in her eyes. "Yes, I remember," she said contemptuously, "the papers tried to hint at some flimsy possibility like that at the time, no doubt deliberately encouraged by you people to cover up your own incompetence. There have been cases before that were never solved—Elwell, Dorothy King, Rothstein—and there's always the same reason; rottenness in the wrong places, bribery in the right places, pull. But there never was a case in the whole history of the police force that was allowed to pass so unnoticed as this. Not even a suspect questioned in it from first to last. As though a dog had been shot down in the streets!"

"As far as our encouraging the papers at the time goes, it was the other way around. We did everything we could to keep them from mentioning the man-across-the-way angle, deliberately misled them with stories of a stray shot from some rooftop, hoping if we kept quiet about it, if this unknown gunman thought he wasn't suspected, it would be easier to get our hands on him."

"I didn't believe it then, and I don't believe it now! I saw with my own eyes——"

"What you saw was an optical illusion, then. If you had come to us at the time, asked us how we were progressing, we could have proved it to your satisfaction once and for all. But no, you hugged your vengeance to yourself, nursed your bitterness, wouldn't interview the police. You deliberately withheld the information that was in your own possession— inaccurate though it was—and used it for murder."

She flashed him a look that was a complacent admission.

"There were powder burns found on the window curtains in that room opposite the church. There were people in it, on the floor above, who distinctly heard a shot beneath their feet, over and above all the backfiring outside. They were in a better position to judge, after all, than you. We even found a discharged shell, of the same caliber as that taken out of your husband's body, wedged between a crack in the floorboards. We knew from the start where the death shot had been fired from; that was why we didn't have to go tracing wild cars all over the city. We knew everything but who the killer was. We only found that out now, recently. Don't you want to know who he is? Don't you at least want to hear his name?"

"Why should I be interested in what rabbits you pull from a trick hat to try to mislead me?"

"The proof is in our files right now. It came in too late to save Bliss, Mitchell, Moran or Ferguson. But it's there today. Scientific proof; proof that cannot be gotten around. Documentary proof; a signed confession—I have a copy with me in my own pocket at this very minute. He's been in custody down in the city for the past three weeks."

For the first time, she had no challenging answer to make.

"You'll meet him face to face when you go back there with me shortly. I think that you'll remember meeting him before."

The first superficial crack had appeared on the glaze that protected her. A flicker of doubt, of dread, peered from her eyes. A question forced its way out. "Who?"

"Corey. Does the name mean anything to you?"

She said with painful slowness, "Yes, I remember this Corey. Twice he crossed my path, for a moment only. Once, on a terrace at a party, he brought me a drink. It would have been so easy to. . . . But I sent him away, to clear the deck for . . ."

"The murder of Bliss, isn't that right?"

"According to you, someone who had never harmed me, never even seen me before that night." She held her forehead briefly, resumed: "And the second and last time, I was up in his very room with him, for a few minutes. I went back to his apartment with him as the simplest way of getting rid of him. I remember I even held him at the point of a gun to make sure of getting out again unhindered. *His* gun."

"The gun that killed your husband. The gun that fired the bullet into Nick Killeen. Through a slip-up on the part of a rookie it was checked by ballistics instead of by the fingerprint department for *your* prints, which was what he had brazenly turned it over to us for.

"I remember I was sitting there raising cain with the fingerprint bureau for not sending me a report on a weapon that had never reached them, when someone at ballistics telephoned me

and said, 'That gun you sent us to be tested matches the mark-
ings on the slug taken out of Nick Killeen; we suppose that's
what you wanted, you weren't very definite about it.' I had to see
it with my own eyes before I'd believe them. Then just to make
the irony all of a piece, Corey comes walking in to find out if we
were through with the gun and he could have it back again. He
never got out again!

"He'd come forward to help us of his own accord. He had
a license for the gun; he was only too willing to let us have
it, to see if we could get your prints off it. I suppose by then
so many years had passed since the Killeen killing, his sense
of immunity had become almost a fetish. He thought nothing
could. . . .

"It took a little while, but we finally broke him down. In
the meantime I had been working independently on what we
all thought was an entirely different matter and came across an
obscure item in old newspapers at the library, datelined on one
of those Fridays that the Friday-Night Fiends had been on the
loose. Just a little human-interest thing, tragic to those immediately involved but not particularly important. A bridegroom had
been struck dead by a stray shot, presumably fired from some
roof nearby, as he was leaving the very church he'd just been
married in.

"To me that story offered the only possible reason for the
murders of the Friday-Night Fiends, who had already lost three
charter members and the bartender they carried around with
them on those tears of theirs. I put two and two together. No
mention was made of who the bereaved bride was, but after all
there must have been one; a man doesn't marry himself.

"So we soft-pedaled Corey's arrest, held him practically in-
communicado, to be sure you wouldn't get wind of it and pull

your next and last punch. It was easy to figure out where it would land, so I simply got into position under it.

"But what I can't figure out is what you did with yourself between visitations, so to speak. How you were able to vanish so completely each time, effect all these quick changes of coiffure and personality. I knew you were coming but to the last minute didn't know from where or how. It was like trying to come to grips with a wraith."

The woman answered abstractedly, "There was nothing very supernatural about it. I suppose you looked for me in out-of-the-way hiding places, rooming houses, cheap hotels. I came into contact with dozens of people daily who never gave me a second look. I lived in a hospital, I'll give you the name if you want, one of the biggest in the city. I worked there and lived right there, didn't have to go out. My hair was kept covered, so no one knew—or cared—what color it was, from first to last. When I was off duty I stayed in my room, didn't encourage friendship from the staff. When it came time to— strike again, I would get a short leave of absence, go away, return again a few days later.

"All for what? All for nothing."

She was breathing again with difficulty, as she had in the chair before.

As though something inside her were breaking up, clogging her windpipe. "So I held the very gun he killed Nick with, in my own hands! Had him helpless at the point of it; lowered it and walked out, to go and kill an innocent man." She began to shiver uncontrollably, as though she had a chill. "Now I can hear that awful cry of Bliss's as he went over the terrace. I didn't hear it then. Now I can hear Mitchell's groan. I can hear them all!"

She bowed her head as abruptly as though her neck had

snapped. Her sobbing was low pitched but intense, even paced as the pulsing of a dynamo.

A long time after, when it had ended, she looked up again. "What did he do it for—Corey, I mean?" she asked. "I must know that."

Paper rattled under his coat. He took out a copy of the confession, unfolded it, offered it to her.

She glanced only at the beginning and at the signature at the end of the last page. Then she returned it. "You tell me," she said. "I believe you now. You are an honest man."

"They were working a racket together, your husband and Corey. A nice, profitable, juicy little racket. The details are here in his confession." He broke off short. "Did Killeen ever tell you that?" he asked.

She nodded. "Yes, he told me. I knew. He told me—all but the names. He told me what would happen to him if he quit. I didn't believe him. I wasn't as familiar with violence then. I told him it was either that or me. I didn't think it was as serious as all that, I didn't believe it could be. You see, I loved him. He took a week or two to make up his mind, and then he made his choice. Me."

For the first time Julie Killeen looked directly at Wanger. She spoke quietly, as though telling him some other woman's story. "He changed his quarters. Our meetings became furtive. I suggested that we go to the police for protection, but he told me he was in it as deep as whoever it was he feared. He said we'd go away. We'd go away *fast*, right from the church door straight to the ship. That was another thing I insisted on, a church wedding." She smiled grimly. "You see, I killed him, in a way. That made my obligation even greater afterward." She hesitated a moment, weary, then went on.

"He said we wouldn't come back right away. Maybe we wouldn't come back for a long time after. He was right. We went away all right—but not together. And we neither of us ever came back again.

"I knew I had to take him on those terms or not at all. There was never much question of a choice in it for me. I wanted him. Lord, how I wanted him. I used to lie awake at nights breaking down the time there still was to go without him into minutes and seconds. It made it seem shorter that way. His business. . . ." She shrugged. "He promised he'd give it up. That was all my conscience was strong enough to demand."

"The mistake you both made," Wanger mused almost to himself, "was in thinking that there's ever any quitting the game he was in. They'd chalked up several killings behind them in the course of 'business.' And then there was the question of the final division of the profits, which is always the main rub. Corcy couldn't let him go. They had each other deadlocked."

The woman interrupted. There was fury in her quiet voice.

"*He* quit. He not only quit but made himself over. Mr. Corey, the dashing man-about-town. That's what he's become! Why couldn't he have let Nick go? Why did he have to kill him?"

For the first time in his career Wanger was answering questions instead of asking them. There was a quality of despair in Julie Killeen that carried them both outside the rules of captive and captor.

"Yes, Corey quit. But by the time he tried it there was no one left to reckon with but himself, don't forget. When Kilieen tried it, there was still Corey. And the way he did it wasn't any too reassuring. Just broke the connection off short, put himself out of reach—probably listening to your well-meant advice—but with enough on Corey to send him to the chair in three or four round trips. Not to mention several thousand dollars that Corey thought was coming to him. Corey had his reasons, all right. He wouldn't have known a moment's peace from then on. There would have been an ax hanging over him every minute of his life. He went out to get Nick while the getting was good, before Killeen got him first. The church was the only place Corey would be sure to find him. Before that, Nick evidently didn't show himself."

"He laid low, very low," she said quietly, almost indifferently.

"Nick had moved. Corey didn't know who the girl was, where she lived."

"We met in the dark in the movies, always two seats in the last row."

"But he finally thought of a way. He went around to all the churches asking questions. Somebody slipped up, and he found out where and when the wedding was going to take place. Then he rented a room that commanded the side entrance. He knew Killeen would use the side entrance. He took a gun in there with him, and a package of food, and he didn't go away from that window for forty-eight hours straight. He figured the time of the ceremony might be moved up at the last minute as a precaution."

There was silence in the room. Wanger thought of the bullet that had killed Nick Killeen, the bullet that had gone over the heads of five other men and yet had inevitably caused the death of four of them. He sighed and looked at Julie Killeen.

"You—he never knew who you were from first to last. You were just that unimportant little white doll-like figure next to his target. And he—you never knew who he was either, did you—the man who took you to his room one night, the man who had killed your husband?"

The woman didn't answer, didn't seem to hear.

"Afterward, he sent a wreath to the funeral, in care of the warden of the church."

The woman shivered, put up a hand as though Wanger had struck her. He saw that he had convinced her at last.

He got up, put the manacle around her wrist, closing it almost gently, as if trying not to disturb her bitter reverie. She seemed not to notice it.

"Let's go," he said gruffly.

She stood up, suddenly became conscious of the steel that linked their wrists. She looked at Wanger and nodded gravely.

"Yes," said Julie Killeen, "it's time for me to go."

THE END

DISCUSSION QUESTIONS

- Eddie Muller calls Cornell Woolrich "the most noir writer in the mystery genre." What in this book would you characterize as noir?

- Consider the structure of the book's plot. How did it add to the suspense of the narrative?

- What did you think of the murder methods used in the novel?

- Did any aspects of the plot date the story? If so, which ones?

- Would the story be different if it were set in the present day? If so, how?

- If you've read other books by Cornell Woolrich, how does this one compare?

- Are there any present-day writers whose work reminds you of Woolrich's?

- If you've seen the film based on this book, discuss the adaptation. What stayed the same? What changed?

AMERICAN MYSTERY CLASSICS *from*

*Available now
in hardcover and paperback:*

Charlotte Armstrong . . . . *The Chocolate Cobweb*

Charlotte Armstrong . . . . *The Unsuspected*

Anthony Boucher. . . . . *Rocket to the Morgue*

Anthony Boucher. . . . . *The Case of the Baker Street Irregulars*

John Dickson Carr. . . . . *The Crooked Hinge*

John Dickson Carr. . . . . *The Mad Hatter Mystery*

Mignon G. Eberhart. . . . . *Murder by an Aristocrat*

Erle Stanley Gardner . . . . *The Case of the Careless Kitten*

Erle Stanley Gardner . . . . *The Case of the Baited Hook*

Frances Noyes Hart . . . . *The Bellamy Trial*

H.F. Heard. . . . . *A Taste for Honey*

Dorothy B. Hughes . . . . *Dread Journey*

Dorothy B. Hughes . . . . *The So Blue Marble*

W. Bolingbroke Johnson . . . . *The Widening Stain*

Frances & Richard Lockridge. . . . . *Death on the Aisle*

AMERICAN MYSTERY CLASSICS

from

*Available now
in hardcover and paperback:*

John P. Marquand . . . . *Your Turn, Mr. Moto*

Stuart Palmer . . . . *The Puzzle of the Happy Hooligan*

Ellery Queen . . . . *The Egyptian Cross Mystery*

Ellery Queen . . . . *The Siamese Twin Mystery*

Patrick Quentin . . . . *A Puzzle for Fools*

Clayton Rawson . . . . *Death From a Top Hat*

Craig Rice . . . . *Home Sweet Homicide*

Mary Roberts Rinehart . . . . *The Haunted Lady*

Mary Roberts Rinehart . . . . *Miss Pinkerton*

Mary Roberts Rinehart . . . . *The Red Lamp*

Joel Townsley Rogers . . . . *The Red Right Hand*

Vincent Starrett . . . . *The Great Hotel Murder*

Cornell Woolrich . . . . *Waltz into Darkness*

And More! Turn the page to learn about some recent releases...

Visit penzlerpublishers.com, email info@penzlerpublishers.com for
more information, or find us on social media at @penzlerpub

Charlotte Armstrong
The Unsuspected

Introduction by Otto Penzler

*To catch a murderous theater impresario, a young
woman takes a deadly new role . . .*

The note discovered beside Rosaleen Wright's hanged body is full of reasons justifying her suicide—but it lacks her trademark vitality and wit, and, most importantly, her signature. So the note alone is far from enough to convince her best friend Jane that Rosaleen was her own murderer, even if the police quickly accept the possibility as fact. Instead, Jane suspects Rosaleen's boss, Luther Grandison. To the world at large, he's a powerful and charismatic figure, directing for stage and screen, but Rosaleen's letters to Jane described a duplicitous, greedy man who would no doubt kill to protect his secrets. Jane and her friend Francis set out to infiltrate Grandy's world and collect evidence, employing manipulation, impersonation, and even gaslighting to break into his inner circle. But will they recognize what dangers lie therein before it's too late?

CHARLOTTE ARMSTRONG (1905-1969) was an American author of mystery short stories and novels. Having started her writing career as a poet and dramatist, she wrote a few novels before *The Unsuspected*, which was her first to achieve outstanding success, going on to be adapted for film by Michael Curtiz.

"Psychologically rich, intricately plotted and full of
dark surprises, Charlotte Armstrong's suspense tales feel
as vivid and fresh today as a half century ago."
—Megan Abbott

Paperback, $15.95 / ISBN 978-1-61316-123-4
Hardcover, $25.95 / ISBN 978-1-61316-122-7

Dorothy B. Hughes
Dread Journey

Introduction by
Sarah Weinman

A movie star fears for her life on a train journey from Los Angeles to New York...

Hollywood big-shot Vivien Spender has waited ages to produce the work that will be his masterpiece: a film adaptation of Thomas Mann's The Magic Mountain. He's spent years grooming young starlets for the lead role, only to discard each one when a newer, fresher face enters his view. Afterwards, these rejected women all immediately fall from grace; excised from the world of pictures, they end up in rehab, or jail, or worse. But Kitten Agnew, the most recent to encounter this impending doom, won't be gotten rid of so easily—her contract simply doesn't allow for it. Accompanied by Mr. Spender on a train journey from Los Angeles to Chicago, she begins to fear that the producer might be considering a deadly alternative. Either way, it's clear that something is going to happen before they reach their destination, and as the train barrels through America's heartland, the tension accelerates towards an inescapable finale.

DOROTHY B. HUGHES (1904–1993) was a mystery author and literary critic famous for her taut thrillers, many of which were made into films. While best known for the noir classic *In a Lonely Place*, Hughes' writing successfully spanned a range of styles including espionage and domestic suspense.

"The perfect in-flight read. The only thing that's dated is the long-distance train."—*Kirkus*

Paperback, $15.95 / ISBN 978-1-61316-146-3
Hardcover, $25.95 / ISBN 978-1-61316-145-6

Ellery Queen
The Siamese Twin Mystery

Introduction by Otto Penzler

Ellery Queen takes refuge from a wildfire at a remote mountain house — and arrives just before the owner is murdered...

When Ellery Queen and his father encounter a raging forest fire during a mountain drive, the only direction to go is up a winding dirt road that leads to an isolated hillside manor, inhabited by a secretive surgeon and his diverse cast of guests. Trapped by the fire, the Queens settle into the uneasy atmosphere of their surroundings. Then, the following morning, the doctor is discovered dead, apparently shot down while playing solitaire the night before.

The only clue is a torn six of spades. The suspects include a society beauty, a suspicious valet, and a pair of conjoined twins. When another murder follows, the killer inside the house becomes as threatening as the mortal flames outside its walls. Can Queen solve this whodunnit before the fire devours its subjects?

ELLERY QUEEN was a pen name created and shared by two cousins, Frederic Dannay (1905-1982) and Manfred B. Lee (1905-1971), as well as the name of their most famous detective.

> "Queen at his best . . . a classic of brilliant deduction under extreme circumstances."
> —*Publishers Weekly* (Starred Review)

Paperback, $15.95 / ISBN 978-1-61316-155-5
Hardcover, $25.95 / ISBN   978-1-61316-154-8

OTTO PENZLER PRESENTS
═══AMERICAN MYSTERY CLASSICS═══

Clayton Rawson
Death from a Top Hat

Introduction by Otto Penzler

A detective steeped in the art of magic solves the mystifying murder of two occultists.

Now retired from the tour circuit on which he made his name, master magician The Great Merlini spends his days running a magic shop in New York's Times Square and his nights moonlighting as a consultant for the NYPD. The cops call him when faced with crimes so impossible that they can only be comprehended by a magician's mind.

In the most recent case, two occultists are discovered dead in locked rooms, one spread out on a pentagram, both appearing to have been murdered under similar circumstances. The list of suspects includes an escape artist, a professional medium, and a ventriloquist, so it's clear that the crimes took place in a realm that Merlini knows well. But in the end it will take his logical skills, and not his magical ones, to apprehend the killer.

CLAYTON RAWSON (1906–1971) was a novelist, editor, and magician. He is best known for creating the Great Merlini, an illusionist and amateur sleuth introduced in *Death from a Top Hat* (1938).

> "One of the all-time greatest impossible murder mysteries."
> —*Publishers Weekly* (Starred Review)

Paperback, $15.95 / ISBN 978-1-61316-101-2
Hardcover, $25.95 / ISBN 978-1-61316-109-8

Craig Rice
Home Sweet Homicide

Introduction by Otto Penzler

The children of a mystery writer play amateur sleuths and matchmakers

Unoccupied and unsupervised while mother is working, the children of widowed crime writer Marion Carstairs find diversion wherever they can. So when the kids hear gunshots at the house next door, they jump at the chance to launch their own amateur investigation—and after all, why shouldn't they? They know everything the cops do about crime scenes, having read about them in mother's novels. They know what her literary detectives would do in such a situation, how they would interpret the clues and handle witnesses. Plus, if the children solve the puzzle before the cops, it will do wonders for the sales of mother's novels. But this crime scene isn't a game at all; the murder is real and, when its details prove more twisted than anything in mother's fiction, they'll eventually have to enlist Marion's help to sort out the clues. Or is that just part of their plan to hook her up with the lead detective on the case?

CRAIG RICE (1908–1957), born Georgiana Ann Randolph Craig, was an American author of mystery novels, short stories, and screenplays. Rice's writing style was unique in its ability to mix gritty, hard-boiled writing with the entertainment of a screwball comedy.

"A genuine midcentury classic."—*Booklist*

Paperback, $15.95 / ISBN 978-1-61316-103-6

Hardcover, $25.95 / ISBN 978-1-61316-112-8

Cornell Woolrich
Waltz into Darkness

Introduction by
Wallace Stroby

From "the supreme master of suspense" comes the chilling chronicle of one man's descent into madness. (New York Times)

When New Orleans coffee merchant Louis Durand first meets his bride-to-be after a months-long courtship by mail, he's shocked that she doesn't match the photographs sent with her correspondence. But Durand has told his own fibs, concealing from her the details of his wealth, and so he mostly feels fortunate to find her so much more beautiful than expected. Soon after they marry, however, he becomes increasingly convinced that the woman in his life is not the same woman with whom he exchanged letters, a fact that becomes unavoidable when she suddenly disappears with his fortune.

Alone, desperate, and inexplicably love-sick, Louis quickly descends into madness, obsessed with finding Julia and bringing her to justice—and simply with seeing her again. He engages the services of a private detective to do so, embarking on a search that spans the southeast of the country. When he finally tracks her down, the nightmare truly begins…

CORNELL WOOLRICH (1903–1968) was one of America's best crime fiction writers. Famous for suspenseful and dark plots, his work inspired more films noir than that of any other author.

"A richly embroidered tapestry … this is classic noir well worthy of a revival"—*Booklist*

Paperback, $15.95 / ISBN 978-1-61316-152-4

Hardcover, $25.95 / ISBN 978-1-61316-151-7